NIGHTWING

BATMAN ADVENTURES

TY TEMPLETON
original series and collection cover artist

BATMAN created by BOB KANE with BILL FINGER
NIGHTWING created by MARV WOLFMAN and GEORGE PÉREZ

RISING

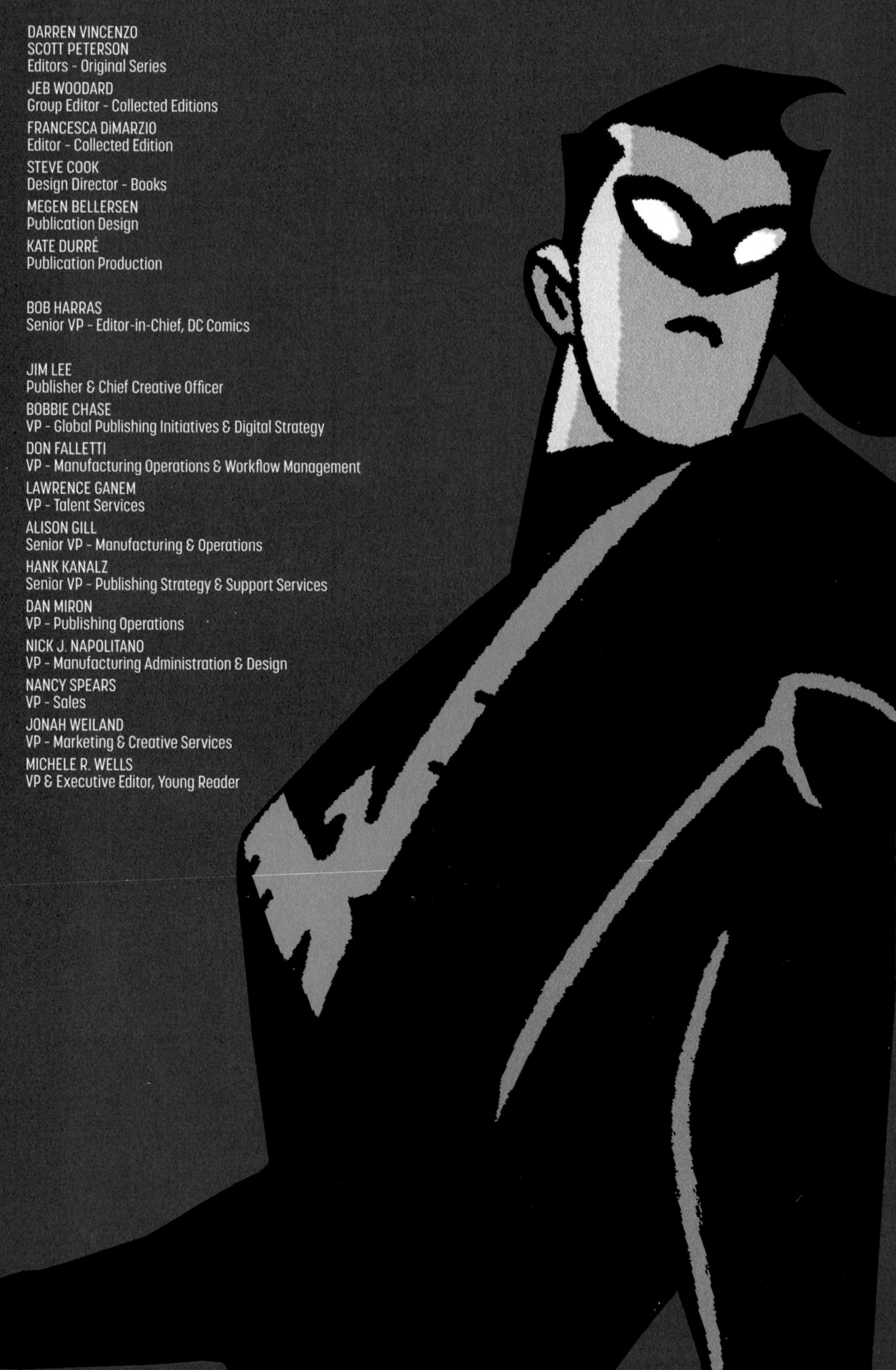

DARREN VINCENZO
SCOTT PETERSON
Editors - Original Series
JEB WOODARD
Group Editor - Collected Editions
FRANCESCA DiMARZIO
Editor - Collected Edition
STEVE COOK
Design Director - Books
MEGEN BELLERSEN
Publication Design
KATE DURRÉ
Publication Production

BOB HARRAS
Senior VP - Editor-in-Chief, DC Comics

JIM LEE
Publisher & Chief Creative Officer
BOBBIE CHASE
VP - Global Publishing Initiatives & Digital Strategy
DON FALLETTI
VP - Manufacturing Operations & Workflow Management
LAWRENCE GANEM
VP - Talent Services
ALISON GILL
Senior VP - Manufacturing & Operations
HANK KANALZ
Senior VP - Publishing Strategy & Support Services
DAN MIRON
VP - Publishing Operations
NICK J. NAPOLITANO
VP - Manufacturing Administration & Design
NANCY SPEARS
VP - Sales
JONAH WEILAND
VP - Marketing & Creative Services
MICHELE R. WELLS
VP & Executive Editor, Young Reader

CONTENTS

NIGHTWING

BATMAN ADVENTURES: NIGHTWING RISING

Published by DC Comics.

DC Comics, 2900 West Alameda Ave., Burbank, CA 91505
Printed by LSC Communications, Crawfordsville, IN, USA. 8/28/20. First Printing.
ISBN: 978-1-77950-722-8

Library of Congress Cataloging-in-Publication Data is available.

PEFC Certified
This product is from sustainably managed forests and controlled sources
PEFC
PEFC/29-31-337
www.pefc.org

NIGHTWING

CHAPTER 1: LOST YEARS

NIGHTWING

NIGHTWING

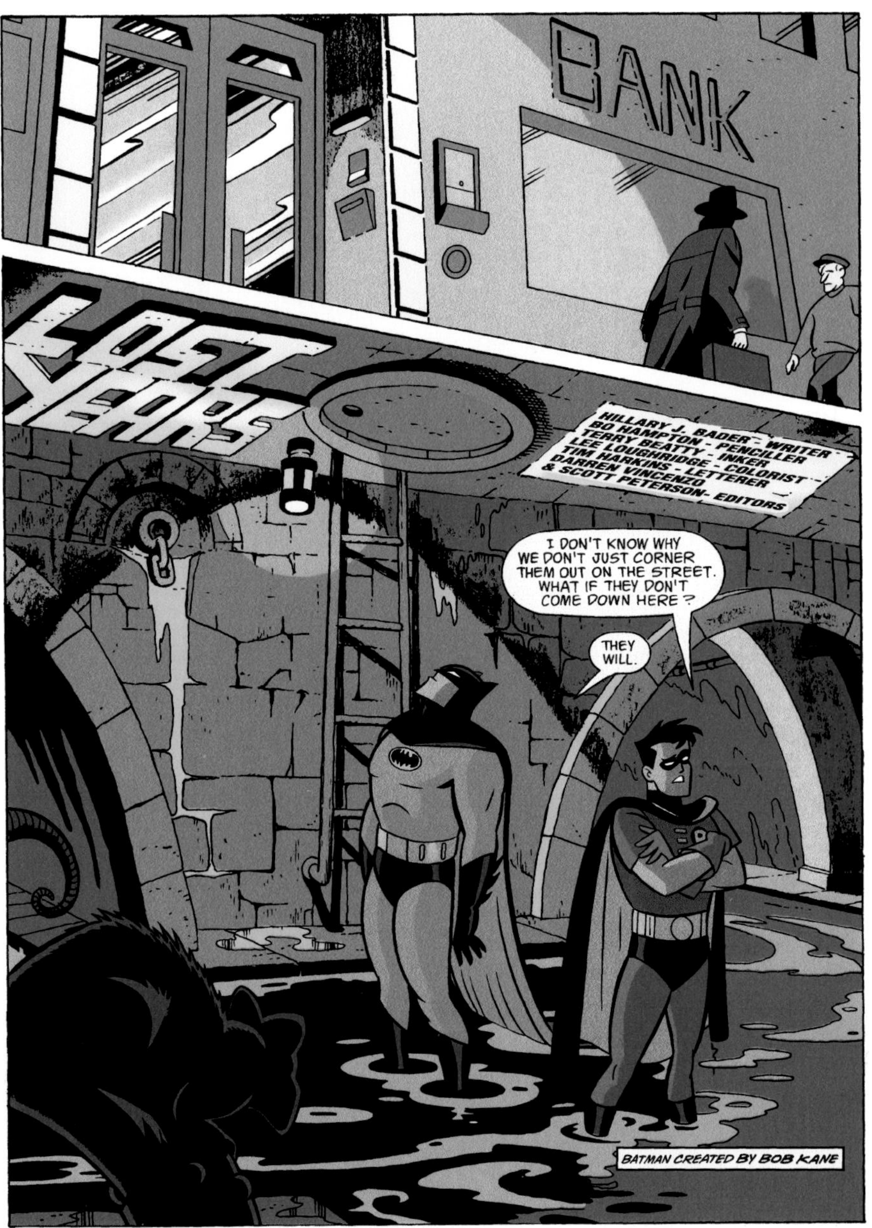
BANK
LOST YEARS
HILLARY J. BADER - WRITER
BO HAMPTON - PENCILLER
TERRY BEATTY - INKER
LEE LOUGHRIDGE - COLORIST
TIM HARKINS - LETTERER
DARREN VINCENZO
& SCOTT PETERSON- EDITORS
I DON'T KNOW WHY WE DON'T JUST CORNER THEM OUT ON THE STREET. WHAT IF THEY DON'T COME DOWN HERE?
THEY WILL.
BATMAN CREATED BY BOB KANE

BANK
THAT'S OUR CUE. LET'S GO.

THEY'RE HEADING SOUTH, ON FOOT.
I SHOULD'VE WORN MY WATERPROOF BOOTS.
SHOULD'VE. COULD'VE.

THIS IS THE ONE.
HOW CAN YOU BE SURE?

ARE YOU GOING TO QUESTION EVERYTHING I TELL YOU?
NOW MAKE YOURSELF PART OF THE WALLS.

THERE IT IS.

COPS ARE COMIN'.

WHO CARES? AS LONG AS THE BAT AIN'T HERE BY NOW, WE'RE HOME FREE.

DID YOU CLOSE THE COVER?
I DO MY JOB!
HEY! (SNIFF SNIFF) WHAT'S THAT SMELL?

HUMAN VERMIN!
THE BAT!

WHAT'S YOUR RUSH?

OOF
ROBIN--
LOOK
OUT!
LOOK OUT
YOURSELF!
UNGH.
ROBIN! NO!
I CAN
HANDLE
HIM!
IT'S A
DEAD
END!
I SAID
I CAN---

SHOULDA LISTENED, KID!
UNGH!
SAY GOODNIGHT, BIRD BOY!
YOU SAY GOODNIGHT!
OUCH!
BATGIRL --- OOOF!
THAT'S MY NAME -- DON'T WEAR IT OUT!

OOF!
AIN'T SO SMART-MOUTH NOW.

OOF!
GEE --
I WISH I COULD THINK OF SOMETHING WITTY.
UGH!

THAT'S THIRTY LOVE.
YOU'RE ENJOYING THIS.
OF COURSE I AM.

FORTY.
NO FAIR. YOU PLAYED VARSITY.

I *WON* VARSITY.
AND THAT'S CALLED *GAME!*

NICE WORK.
CARE FOR ANOTHER?
DICK LOOKS TUCKERED OUT.

YOU THINK YOU CAN DO BETTER?
WELL... YES...
ALWAYS A FRESH CHICKEN TO BE PLUCKED.
LET'S DO IT.

NICE, BUT YOU'LL HAVE TO DO BETTER THAN THAT.
THWOK

HNNNG! LUCKY SHOT.
THWOK

THWOK
ANOTHER LUCKY SHOT.

I BELIEVE THAT'S *GAME*.
THWOK

I'M IMPRESSED. NOT MANY PEOPLE CAN BEAT ME ON THE COURT. HOW'D YOU DO IT ?
EASY. I WAS WATCHING YOU. WHENEVER YOU GO TO YOUR *LEFT* YOU LEAVE YOUR *RIGHT* SIDE---
HMMM.
MY RIGHT SIDE ?

---YOUR RIGHT SIDE OPEN.
SO, ARE YOU READY FOR GRADUATION TOMORROW...

..."MISTER GRAYSON"?
READY AS I'LL EVER BE.
AT LEAST YOU'LL HAVE TIME TO WORK ON YOUR TENNIS GAME.

I ASSUME YOU'LL BE THERE WITH BELLS ON.
I CAN'T IMAGINE WHAT WOULD KEEP ME AWAY.

CLASS OF 1997
ANDREW GOODWIN.
CLAPCLAPCLA

YOU MUST BE VERY PROUD OF DICK...
RICHARD GRAYSON, WITH HIGHEST HONORS.
HE'LL BE CRUSHED THAT BRUCE MISSED THIS.
CLAP-LAPCLAP

...AND NO MORE SPONGING OFF BRUCE.
Oh, A VOW OF POVERTY?

NO, I'VE GOT A TRUST FUND FROM THE CIRCUS.
BUT WHATEVER MY FUTURE HOLDS, I HOPE IT WILL INCLUDE YOU.
BEEPBEEPBEEP

EXCUSE ME, I HAVE TO TAKE THIS.

THIS ISN'T A GREAT TIME.
I'M NOT MAKING THE SCHEDULE.
RIGHT.
EXCUSE ME, MISS, BUT WILL THE YOUNG MAN BE RETURNING?
I'M AFRAID HE HAD SOMETHING MORE "IMPORTANT" TO DO.
"CLEAN OUT THE FRIDGE." WHAT KIND OF AN EXCUSE IS--
ATTENTION ALL CARS. SILENT ALARM AVATECH LABS NEAR DECKER AND FIFTH.
HUH?
PROCEED WITH CAUTION.
DECKER AND FIFTH, HUH?
GLAD I GOT THAT POLICE BAND RADIO.
AND A CHANGE OF CLOTHES.

YOU'RE LATE.
EXCUSE ME FOR HAVING A LIFE.
THE JOKER IS DOWN THERE.
WELL, WHAT ARE WE WAITING FOR?

HEADS UP!
RATATATATAT
NICE ENTRANCE...

TIME TO FLY!
BATMAN! oh NO. I'M SUNK. I'M COOKED.

HEY! WHAT ABOUT ME?
SQUUEELL!

YOU CAN RUN, BUT YOU CAN'T HIDE.

SLAM!
JIMMY, WHAT'S WRONG?

OUT THE FIRE ESCAPE. QUICK!

I'LL SAVE YOU, DADDY.
OOOF!
STAY BACK!

WHERE'S JOKER?
I--I DON'T KNOW...

THAT SOUNDED LIKE TROUBLE.
CRASH!

REMEMBER NOW?

DADDY!

BATMAN, NOT LIKE THIS.
NOT IN FRONT OF HIS FAMILY.

THE SOONER HE TALKS, THE BETTER.

I'M OUT OF HERE, NOW!

ROBIN!
DOWN HERE.

WHAT'S WRONG?

WAIT!

ROBIN?
GONE. WHAT'S GOING ON BETWEEN YOU TWO?

I WISH I KNEW.

SO, TELL ME AGAIN WHY WE'RE WAITING HERE.
JIMMY WASN'T ABLE TO GIVE ME THE INFORMATION I NEEDED.

"CAN'T GET BLOOD FROM A STONE"?
SOMETHING LIKE THAT.
BUT UNLESS I MISS MY GUESS, JIMMY'S DUE TO RECEIVE SOME UNEXPECTED VISITORS.

SSLUURP!

SORRY.
SO DO YOU WANT TO TALK ABOUT IT?
WHAT?
YOU AND ROBIN.

SILLY QUESTION.

yawn!
PAST YOUR BEDTIME?
JUST THINKING HOW NICE AND WARM IT MUST BE IN MY NICE COZY APARTMENT.

WHICH WOULD BE WHERE, EXACTLY?

MY, AREN'T WE GETTING UNUSUALLY CURIOUS TONIGHT.
I'LL SHOW YOU MINE IF YOU SHOW ME YOURS.
THAT'S THEM.

ON SECOND THOUGHT, THE MAID HASN'T BEEN IN MY APARTMENT FOR A MONTH. IT'S NOT FIT TO SHOW ANYONE.

THE BOSS SAYS, WHEN JIMMY COMES OUT FOR THE CASH, WE ICE HIM.

BE NICE IF WE COULD MAKE IT LOOK ACCIDENTAL LIKE.

I'M SURE ACCIDENTS CAN BE ARRANGED.

LIGHTS OUT, FELLAS.
BONK
UNGH!
NICE JOB--BUT I WAS PLANNING ON QUESTIONING THEM.
YOU SHOULD HAVE TOLD ME.
YOU'RE RIGHT. I SHOULD HAVE.
I'M GLAD SOMEONE'S STILL WILLING TO TAKE MY ADVICE.
WHAT DO YOU MEAN?
I SEE YOU'RE KEEPING YOUR GUARD UP NOW WHEN YOU GO LEFT.
YEAH, WELL, I DON'T HAVE TO BE TOLD THREE TIMES.

MASTER BRUCE. MISS GORDON IS HERE TO SEE YOU.
BARBARA'S HERE?

IN THE STUDY, SIR.
GOOD. TELL HER I'LL BE RIGHT THERE, ALFRED.

...AND IT WASN'T THE FIRST TIME I'VE SEEN HIM LIKE THAT.
WHAT IS IT BETWEEN YOU TWO? WHAT'S GOING ON?

YOU REALLY CARE FOR HIM, DON'T YOU?

FOLLOW ME.

oh...
oh MY GOD.

MASTER BRUCE, I...
MS. GORDON. I, uh, SEE YOU'VE DISCOVERED OUR LITTLE SECRET.

YES, I ADMIT IT. I AM BATMAN.

IT'S ALL RIGHT, ALFRED.
BUT... WHY WOULD YOU TRUST ME WITH THIS?
FOR DICK'S SAKE. BESIDES, I'M NOT THE ONLY ONE WITH A SECRET. AM I--

BATGIRL.

CHAPTER 2: GRADUATION DAY

NIGHTWING

NIGHTWING

... INTERRUPT TO BRING YOU THIS SPECIAL BULLETIN.

THESE PICTURES WERE WIRED INTO OUR STATION JUST MOMENTS AGO.

MY WORD!

EXCUSE ME, SIR. THIS COMES AT A MOST INOPPORTUNE MOMENT...

GRADUATION DAY

HILARY J. BADER *Writer* · BO HAMPTON *Penciller* · TERRY BEATTY *Inker* · LEE LOUGHRIDGE *Colorist* · TIM HARKINS *Letterer* · DARREN VINCENZO & SCOTT PETERSON *Editors*

Batman created by BOB KANE

THAT'S RIGHT, FRIENDS, THANKS TO THIS SMASHING NEW INVENTION...

CRRASHH!
AUUGHH!
SCHOOL
Old FOLKS HOME
NO MILITARY OR COMMERCIAL PLANES CAN SAFELY FLY OVER GOTHAM.

uh-oh!

ALFRED, CONTACT ROBIN.

I'VE ALREADY TRIED, SIR. I'M AFRAID HE'S NOT ANSWERING.

CLICK

BEEP
BEEP
BEEP
WHAT DOES HE WANT NOW?

THERE'S NOBODY HOME.
CLICK

BEEP
BEEP
BEEP
I SAID THERE'S NOBODY--

--HOME!!
BEEP BEEP
BEEP
MESSAGE
SPLASH!

JUST REMEMBER ONE THING.

I DRIVE THE BATMOBILE.

SQUEEEEEEL!

YOU *DO* KNOW THERE'S A WALL UP AHEAD.

NOT FOR LONG.

YEEEE HA!

117
SLAP
SLAM
UNGH!
THOK

NO MORE, PLEASE!
JUST GIVE UP THE COMBINATION.
YEAH. THE COMBINATION.

BUT I DON'T HAVE IT! REALLY!
THEN I GUESS WE HAVE TO CUT IT OFF.
YEAH. HEH.

OW!
WHAT WAS THAT ?
BRILLIANT MOVE, GRAYSON.
MEOW!

IT AIN'T NOTHIN' BUT A CAT.
JONESY. GO CHECK IT OUT.

TOLD YA. NOTHING BUT A...

...LITTLE OLD CAT.

NOW, WHERE WERE WE?
I THINK I WAS ABOUT TO DO SOME CUTTIN'.
UH... NOW WOULD BE A GOOD TIME.
A GOOD TIME FOR WHAT?
ME.

UNGH!
UNGH!

RIP!
GREAT! MY NEW SHIRT!
NAILS
BATGRAPPLE WOULD HAVE BEEN FASTER.
BUT NO MORE EFFECTIVE.
KRAK!
HEY! LOOK OUT!
THUNK!
HUH!
UNGH.

MAN... NOT MY PANTS, TOO.
OOOF!
RIP!

I SHOULDN'T BE DOING THIS IN MY CIVVIES.
ANGH!

IS EVERYBODY DONE FOR THE NIGHT?

uh, EXCUSE ME.

WHOA! PLEASE DON'T HURT ME!
I'VE GOT KIDS!

I... I'M SORRY. I DIDN'T MEAN...
I THOUGHT...
I UNDERSTAND. ADRENALINE. EXCITEMENT OF THE HUNT.
YOU MUST HAVE BEEN PUMPED. IT'S ALL RIGHT.
NO, IT'S NOT ALL RIGHT!
LOSING IT IS NEVER ALL RIGHT.
ACTING IN ANGER IS WRONG. IT'S WRONG.
I... I JUST WANTED TO THANK YOU AND ALL.
I DON'T DO IT FOR THANKS.
I... I DON'T KNOW WHY I DO IT ANYMORE.
WHAT YOU DID-- IT'S A GOOD THING. YOU WERE A REAL HERO.
BUT I DON'T WANT TO BE A HERO. I WANT TO BE AN ORDINARY GUY.
I WANT A WIFE. KIDS. I WON'T BE LIKE HIM.
I WON'T.

THE JOKER HAS TO SET THE DISRUPTER AT THE HIGHEST POINT IN GOTHAM.
THAT KIND OF NARROWS DOWN OUR CHOICES TO JUST ONE.

"THE GOTHAM EMPIRE STATE BUILDING!"
READY TO FLY, CAP'N.
CONTACT! HA HA HA HAHAHA.

THE STAIRWAYS ARE SEALED OFF AND THERE'S GAS BOMBS IN THE ELEVATOR SHAFTS.
HAHAHAHAHA
CLICK

NO WAY ANYONE'S GETTIN' TO US UP HERE.
IZZAT SO?

BATS IN OUR BELFRY AGAIN!
OOF!

SWACK!

OW!

OOH, SOMETHING NEW HAS BEEN ADDED.

A BIG IMPROVEMENT OVER THE BOY BLUNDER!

HA HA HA HA HA

RRIIPP!

FUNNY, BARBARA DIDN'T SAY ANYTHING ABOUT COMING BY.
VROOOOM!

BARBARA!
ALFRED!
BRUCE?
WHERE IS EVERYBODY?

ALFRED, I SAW BARBARA'S CAR PARKED OUT FRONT...
WHERE IS SHE?

WBIX EVENING NEWS
GOTHAM TONIGHT
SHE AND MASTER BRUCE ARE RUNNING AN ERRAND.
WHAT KIND OF ERRAND?
UM...

WHERE DID THEY GO?

OOOF.
MY, SHE'S A FEISTY LITTLE MINX.
AND QUITE A LOOKER, TOO.
UNGH!
WHACK!
STILL, BUSINESS IS BUSINESS.
APIRE
BARBARA...
NOOOO!

CLICK!
NOOOO!
FWOOOOOM
OOOF!
THANKS.
WE GOTTA TALK.
NOT NOW. HE NEEDS US.

KILL HIM!
SOUVENIRS
EMPIRE HAT $15. U.S.
MISS ME, FELLAS?
OOOF!
RATA-TAT
YOU SHOULD BE SIDEWALK STROGANOFF.
I CHANGED THE MENU!
MUST I DO EVERYTHING MYSELF?
OOOF!
COOL.

KABOOOM!

HOUSTON, WE HAVE A PROBLEM...

BATGIRL! I STILL CAN'T BELIEVE IT.
HOW COULD YOU KEEP SOMETHING LIKE THIS FROM ME?
YOU WEREN'T EXACTLY HONEST WITH ME EITHER.

BUT YOU TOLD *HIM*.
HE KNEW.
IT WASN'T MY PLACE TO TELL YOU.

BUT IT WAS YOUR PLACE TO PUT HER IN DANGER.
IT WASN'T LIKE THAT.

I VOLUNTEERED.
YOU THINK YOU DID. YOU DON'T KNOW HIM LIKE I DO.

HE MANIPULATES. PULLS STRINGS. ANYTHING TO GET WHAT HE WANTS.
I THOUGHT WE HAD THE SAME GOALS.
GOTHAM
2-NITE

THINGS CHANGE. I CHANGED.
THE GAME'S OVER, BATMAN. I QUIT.

ROBIN, WAIT...

WHACK!

GO AFTER HIM. BRING HIM BACK.
IT'S TOO LATE. MAYBE SOME-DAY BUT NOT NOW.

YES. I NEED TO KNOW THE TOTAL AMOUNT IN THE TRUST FUND.
BECAUSE IT'S *MY* MONEY, AND I NEED IT.

WELL, I'M GOING TO NEED IT LIQUID. RIGHT AWAY.

I'M GOING ON A TRIP.
CLICK

I CAN'T JUST LEAVE YOU LYING THERE LIKE THAT.
I NEVER REALIZED HOW BRIGHT YOUR COLORS ARE.

COLORS FOR A CHILD. NOT A MAN.

I CAN'T WEAR YOU. EVER. EVER AGAIN.
I DON'T KNOW WHAT THERE IS FOR ME TO TAKE YOUR PLACE.

BUT I'M GOING TO FIND OUT.

I WISH YOU LUCK, ROB---
DICK.
I HOPE YOU FIND WHAT YOU'RE LOOKING FOR.

CHAPTER 3: NOW YOU SEE 'EM

NIGHTWING

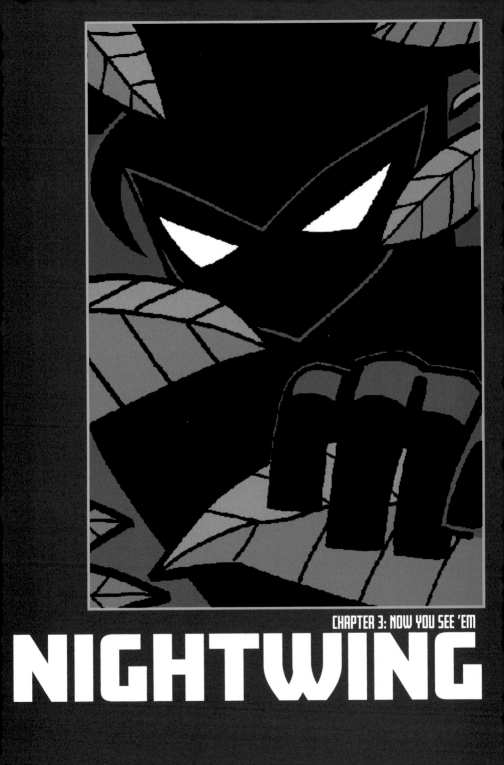

NIGHTWING

São Paolo, Brazil. Day two hundred seventy-nine. Ling Chao told me I lacked fear of heights. That it would either be what made me a great master or it would be my undoing.
He told me that Tai Chi was not going to help me find out which. That I must move on.
Just as well. The weather is better here in Brazil than it was on the Northern Chinese Mongolian border.
And I've found some... new friends to play with...
NOW YOU SEE 'EM
HILARY J. BADER-writer BO HAMPTON-penciller TERRY BEATTY-inker LEE LOUGHRIDGE-colorist
TIM HARKINS-letterer DARREN VINCENZO & SCOTT PETERSON-editors
Batman Created By BOB KANE

They like to play rough.

THWAK
OFF!
UNGH!
I do too.

It's been a real blast playing with the guys, though I'll have a few bruises to remember them by.
Of course, they'll have more to remember me by.
But it is time to move on. No matter how much I've learned from...

...CAPOEIRA!

<SEE JUANITO? THERE'S MORE TO THE MARTIAL ARTS THAN BOOM BANG BIM.>
<YOU'RE A BORN PERFORMER. YOU SHOULD STAY WITH US. BECOME A CAPOEIRISTA MASTER.>
<HO HO, FREDERICO. DON'T BE PUTTING IDEAS IN JUANITO'S HEAD. HE ALREADY THINKS HE'S A MASTER.>
<I CAN'T STAY, FREDERICO, PAOLO. I HAVE TO MOVE ON.>

<HE IS ALWAYS THINKING ABOUT THE NEXT MASTER. THE NEXT TEACHER. ISN'T THAT TRUE> "SEÑOR JOHN SMITH"?
<I... I'M JUST TRYING TO LEARN ALL I CAN.>
<BUT YOU'RE TRYING TO LEARN IT ALL SO FAST. TAKE YOUR TIME, JUANITO. LEARN SOMETHING ABOUT YOURSELF IN THE PROCESS.>

AUTOBUS
<SO, YOU'RE GOING TO SANTO DE LA ROSA?>
<I DON'T KNOW WHY ANYONE WOULD WANT TO GO TO THAT DUNGHEAP OF A COUNTRY.>
<I KNOW WHY! LOS INVISIBALES!
<THE INVISIBLE TRIBE. YOU WANT TO LEARN THEIR SECRETS.>

<AND I THOUGHT I WAS GULLIBLE. THERE IS NO SUCH TRIBE, JUANITO.>
<HOW DO YOU KNOW?>
<NO ONE HAS EVER SEEN THEM.>

<NO ONE HAS SEEN THEM BECAUSE THEY KNOW HOW TO BECOME INVISIBLE. BESIDES, PEOPLE HAVE HAD GLIMPSES OF THEM.>
<WELL, IF YOU'RE GOING TO SANTO DE LA ROSA THIS TIME OF YEAR, YOU'RE GOING TO NEED THIS.>
<IT'S ENOUGH TO GET YOU STARTED.>

<TELL THE OTHERS I SAID GOOD-BYE. AND TELL THE MASTER THAT... I WILL USE WHAT HE TAUGHT ME WELL.>
<WE KNOW THAT ALREADY> "JOHN SMITH."

WHAT IS THIS SUPPOSED TO MEAN?
<I SEE YOU ARE HEADING TO SANTO DE LA ROSA, ALSO, SEÑOR.>

<HOW DID YOU--->
<OH! YES I AM.>
<IS THIS YOUR FIRST VISIT THERE?>
<YES.>

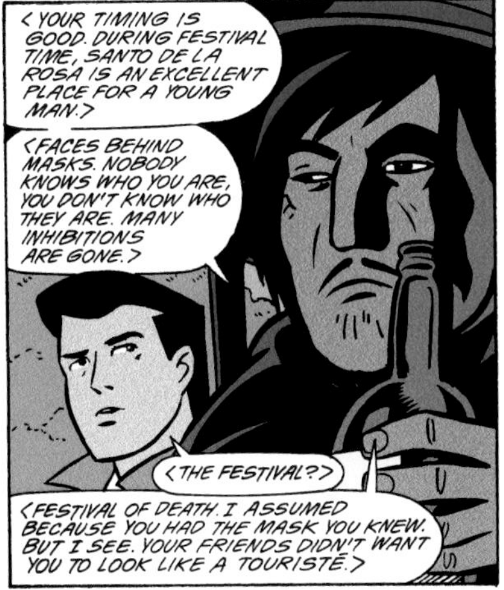
<YOUR TIMING IS GOOD. DURING FESTIVAL TIME, SANTO DE LA ROSA IS AN EXCELLENT PLACE FOR A YOUNG MAN.>
<FACES BEHIND MASKS. NOBODY KNOWS WHO YOU ARE, YOU DON'T KNOW WHO THEY ARE. MANY INHIBITIONS ARE GONE.>
<THE FESTIVAL?>
<FESTIVAL OF DEATH. I ASSUMED BECAUSE YOU HAD THE MASK YOU KNEW. BUT I SEE. YOUR FRIENDS DIDN'T WANT YOU TO LOOK LIKE A TOURISTÉ.>

<BUT YOU SHOULD GET YOURSELF A COSTUME, TOO.>
ALTO

<BUY A COSTUME, SEÑOR?>
<NOT NOW, THANK YOU.>
<YOU WILL NEED A HOTEL, NO? MY COUSIN RUNS THE BEST HOTEL IN SANTO DE LA ROSA. OFF THE BEATEN TRACK, AS YOU WOULD SAY.>

<I AM RODRIGUEZ. I AM AT YOUR SERVICE.>
<WELL, I'M NOT PLANNING ON STAYING LONG. JUST LONG ENOUGH TO FIND A GUIDE INTO THE RAIN FOREST, NEAR THE VENTURA RIVER.>

<NO, SEÑOR. YOU DON'T WANT TO GO THERE.>
<BECAUSE OF THE INVISIBLES?>
<HAHAHA, SEÑOR. THAT IS AN OLD LOCAL MYTH. I DON'T BELIEVE IN FAIRY STORIES ANYMORE.>

<NO, SEÑOR. WHEN I WAS YOUNG IT WAS A SAFE PLACE. BUT THERE ARE FACTORIES IN THE JUNGLE NOW.>
<PLACES A TOURISTÉ LIKE YOURSELF WILL NOT FIND A WARM WELCOME.>
<FACTORIES THAT MAKE WHAT?>

<I HAVE SAID TOO MUCH ALREADY. COME. YOU WILL WANT A SHOWER.>
<YOU LOOK LIKE A LAD WHO CAN TAKE A COLD SHOWER. MY COUSIN'S HOTEL HAS NO HOT WATER.>
<BUT OTHERWISE, IT IS THE BEST HOTEL IN SANTO DE LA ROSA.>

Day two hundred eighty-five. Santo de la Rosa. Rodriguez says I can leave my stuff here at his cousin's hotel.
I told him I might be gone for weeks, if I can find a guide. That seems all right with them.
<SEÑOR. THERE ARE DELAYS THAT CAN'T-->
TWO MILLION FOR TWO SHIPMENTS IN TWO MONTHS. NOT SO HARD TO UNDERSTAND.
NOW THAT'S A FAMILIAR VOICE.

YOU HAVE TWO CHOICES. EITHER I GET WHAT I WANT, OR YOU GET WHAT YOU DON'T WANT.
I'M GUESSING I'LL FIND THE VOICE COMING FROM A FAMILIAR FACE.
OR SHOULD I SAY "FAMILIAR FACES."

"TWO FACES!"
IF MY MONEY IS FINANCING IT, I WANT TO SEE EVERY DETAIL OF THE OPERATION. INCLUDING THE FACTORY.
< YES. SEÑOR. TOMORROW. >

NOT TOMORROW, MAÑANA-MAN. TODAY! TWO HOURS. I MEET YOU AT THE PLAZA DE INVISIBALES. COMPRENDEZ?
SI, YES, SEÑOR. YO COMPRENDEZ. I UNDERSTAND.

RODRIGUEZ SAYS I LOOK LIKE A TOURISTĒ, STICK OUT LIKE A SORE THUMB.
GOTTA FIND SOME WAY TO BLEND IN, BECOME "INVISIBLE"-- AT LEAST TO TWO-FACE.
PLAZA DE INVISIBALES IN TWO HOURS. THAT SHOULD GIVE ME JUST ENOUGH TIME TO FIND AN APPROPRIATE COSTUME. AFTER ALL, IT'S FESTIVAL -- THE PLACE IS CRAWLING WITH...

<... COSTUMES? YOU WANT, I HAVE. THE OLD ONE. MANY A YOUNG MAN LIKES TO FOOL THE LADIES WITH THIS ONE.>
<THANK YOU, NO. I'LL TAKE THIS ONE.>
<ah, OLD SEÑOR DEATH HIMSELF. YOU WILL SCARE AWAY THE LADIES. BUT... YOU KNOW BEST.>

<YOU WANT TO TRY IT ON? I HAVE A ROOM FOR CHANGING.>
<WHERE?>

<HERE.>
<GO AHEAD--NO ONE CAN SEE. DON'T BE SO MODEST.>
MODEST AND QUICK.

<WELL? WHAT DO YOU THINK?>
<MAYBE YOU WON'T SCARE THE LADIES AWAY.>

OH, GREAT-- HOW AM I GONNA FIND ANYONE?
EVERYBODY'S WEARING A MASK. THEY ALL LOOK THE SAME.
EXCEPT...

WHICH OF THESE THINGS IS NOT LIKE THE OTHER?
UNLESS I MISS MY GUESS, I'VE FOUND TWO-FACE'S HIRED HELP.

TIME TO BLEND IN.

HERE THEY ARE. GET IN. FAST.

YOU BETTER KNOW WHERE THIS FACTORY IS. I DON'T GIVE TWO CHANCES.
<BUT, SÊNOR, I ONLY KNOW HOW TO FIND HER FROM THE GROUND. I DO NOT KNOW IF I CAN FIND IT FROM ABOVE.>
GET IN!
<BUT, SÊNOR, I AM AFRAID. I-->

I DON'T ASK TWICE EITHER.
WE HAVE TWO FACTORIES TO FIND.
I CAN DOUBLE MY TWO MILLION DOLLARS IN TWO MONTHS.
AIIIYYEEE!

I NEVER KNEW TWO-FACE TO BE INTO DRUGS.
I GUESS THE DOUBLE OR NOTHING OFFER WAS TOO MUCH FOR HIM TO TURN DOWN.
WELL, DICK...

...HERE'S HOPING "NO FEAR OF HEIGHTS" DOESN'T GET YOU KILLED.

WHICH WAY?
<I... THINK THERE. NEAR THE MOUNTAIN. THERE IS A STREAM. AND A WATERFALL.>
I CAN SEE THE WATERFALL. TO THE LEFT OR RIGHT?
<THERE SHE IS. THE CLEARING! YOU SEE IT?>

WHAT WAS THAT?
DUNNO. I FELT IT TOO. A WEIGHT SHIFT.
CHANCES ARE IT'S NOTHING.
HAVE IT CHECKED OUT. I DON'T LIKE LEAVING THINGS UP TO CHANCE...

...EXCEPT THE CHANCE OF A COIN TOSS.
YES SIR.
CRACK!
WHAT WAS THAT??

I SAW SOMETHING MOVE OVER THERE. FIND WHATEVER MADE THE NOISE AND KILL IT.
HE WENT THIS WAY.
YOU'RE OUTNUMBERED, GRAYSON.
GONNA HAVE TO GET BY THEM, SOMEHOW.

THERE HE IS!
REALLY, REALLY, REALLY GOTTA WORK ON THOSE STEALTH SKILLS, GRAYSON.

AFTER HIM!
JUNGLE SHOULD PROVIDE SOME COVER.
WHIZZ
WHIZZ
WHIZZ
UNLESS I GET BIT BY A SNAKE OR ATTACKED BY A LION, OR WHATEVER THEY GROW HERE.

WENT THIS WAY.
GREAT. THEY'RE CLOSING IN.
GO AROUND. WE'LL TAKE HIM FROM BOTH DIRECTIONS.
I HATE CLEVER THUGS.

YEESH. I WON'T BITE YOU IF YOU DON'T BITE ME.
I THINK HE WENT THAT WAY.
KEEP GOING THEN.

WHEW. NOW THAT WAS A CLOSE--
uh-oh--
I WON'T YELL OUT LOUD IN SCHOOL. I WON'T YELL OUT LOUD IN SCHOOL. I WON'T YELL OUT LOUD IN SCHOOOOOOO-

SOFT LANDING, GRAYSON. NOW GET UP AND GET OUT OF HERE.
shhhh!

WHO'S THERE? WHO?
TEKA NANA LILLY. PETANOKA. PETANOKA TE DE ACKA BAN.
I... DON'T THINK I HIT MY HEAD.

MY GOD... IT'S THEM.

YOU... YOU'RE THE INVISIBLES. THE INVISIBLE TRIBESMEN.
I'VE... HOW CAN I MAKE YOU UNDERSTAND.
I WANT TO FOLLOW YOU.

TE YAKO MANA HATO.
TE KANA MANA ATO!
THROUGH THIS CLEARING. KEEP LOOKING UP.
HE'S NOT GETTING AWAY THIS TIME. NO PLACE TO GO.

THANK YOU. I THINK YOU UNDERSTAND.
I SEE SOMETHING.

TE YAKO MANA HATO. TE KANA.
RIGHT HERE IS WHERE WE...
HEY, WHAT'S--

I COULD HAVE SWORN...
ah, JUST THE JUNGLE HEAT.
LOS INVISIBALES. THE INVISIBLES. THAT'S WHAT YOU SAW.
YEAH, WHATEVER, SPREAD OUT.

BUT--THEY DIDN'T SEE ME. HOW DID YOU--? I MEAN HOW DID I--
LEARN! TEACH! TEMETANAO!

Day three hundred forty-five. It's been a challenge.
I'm far from understanding how they do what they do. But I'm trying.
At least I have learned better stealth skills. No one will see me unless I want to be seen.
<DID I DO IT, TAGARA?>
<YOU MAKE MUCH NOISE FOR AN INVISIBLE.>
<FRIEND, WHY DO YOU TRY SO HARD WHEN IT IS BEYOND YOU?>
<BECAUSE, TAGARA, I WANT SO MUCH TO LEARN.>
<TO WANT IS NOT TO HAVE THE ABILITY.>
<PERHAPS IT IS NOT IN YOUR BLOOD.>
<PERHAPS THE GODS WILL NOT BLESS YOU AS YOU ARE NOT ONE OF US.>
<IS THAT WHAT YOU THINK, TAGARA?>
<NO. I THINK WE ARE TRAINED FROM BIRTH. AND YOU HAVE COME JUST TOO LATE TO LEARN.>
<BUT YOU HAVE LEARNED MORE THAN ANY OUTSIDER EVER HAS. PERHAPS MORE THAN ANY COULD.>
<TAKE WHAT YOU HAVE LEARNED HERE. USE IT TO BRING GOOD TO YOUR OWN PEOPLE.>
<USE IT TO STOP THOSE MEN WHO WERE AFTER YOU BEFORE THEY HURT SOMEONE. FOR WE COULD TELL, THEY WERE MEN WITH MALICE IN THEIR HEARTS.>
<WE WILL NEVER FORGET YOU, FRIEND OF THE INVISIBLES, NEVER.>

NOR I, YOU, TAGARA. NOR I, YOU.

My time with the invisibales is over. Time once again for me to move on.
But I have some business here in the Rain Forest first.

And once again I have to become a costumed hero to do it.

NOT BAD, GRAYSON, FOR SOMETHING THROWN TOGETHER IN THE MIDDLE OF THE FOREST.
NOW LET'S SEE HOW YOUR STEALTH SKILLS HAVE IMPROVED.

BONK!
SO FAR SO GOOD.

WHAT HAPPENED HERE?

I HAPPENED.
THWAK
CRACK
OOOF!

THIS STUFF HAD BETTER GO OUT TODAY. TWO MONTHS, YOU SAID. AND IT'S BEEN TWO MONTHS!
WHAT WAS THAT?
NOTHING. WE ARE ISOLATED OUT HERE. NO ONE CAN TOUCH US.

BETTER BE NOTHING.
I DON'T LIKE LOSING INVESTMENTS.

GOTTA DESTROY THE DRUGS BEFORE THEY'RE SHIPPED OUT.
BUT I CAN'T START A FIRE IN THE MIDDLE OF A RAIN FOREST.
WATER POWER RUNS THIS ENTIRE FACTORY. THERE MUST BE A TON OF WATER PRESSURE FORCED THROUGH SOME OF THESE PIPES.

GUESS I'LL HAVE TO START A FLOOD.

THERE'S A WATER MAIN BROKEN. IF THIS GETS ANY HIGHER IT'LL DESTROY THE GOODS.
GO TURN OFF THE CUTOFF.
THWOK

HUH?
NO! STOP HIM!
AND GET THE WATER CUT OFF NOW!

SEÑOR. THE MERCHANDISE. SHE IS GETTING WET. IT WILL BE THE END OF HER.
CAN'T ANYBODY SHOOT STRAIGHT ?
WASTED. TWO MONTHS WASTED.
I'M OUTTA HERE.
TEKA TO MANO TE LIKO.
AS MY FRIENDS WOULD SAY.
TWO-FACE!
CRACK!
AT LEAST HE'S GOING BACK TO GOTHAM EMPTY-HANDED.
GOTHAM! SUCH A LONG WAY AWAY. SUCH A LONG TIME AGO.
AND IT'S TIME TO MOVE ON AGAIN.

Day three-hundred-sixty-five. Exactly one year since I left Gotham. I have taken this job in the coal room of the steamer to pay passage back to Asia.
Back to Tibet and cold weather again.

I wish I had caught Two-Face, but I can be satisfied that I stopped the flow of drugs to Gotham, at least for a while.

I don't think the mask will be much help in Tibet.
The suit might be of some value though.

Am I burning too many bridges? Searching for too much?
Was the Wizard of Oz right after all?

One year. I wonder if anyone else remembers.

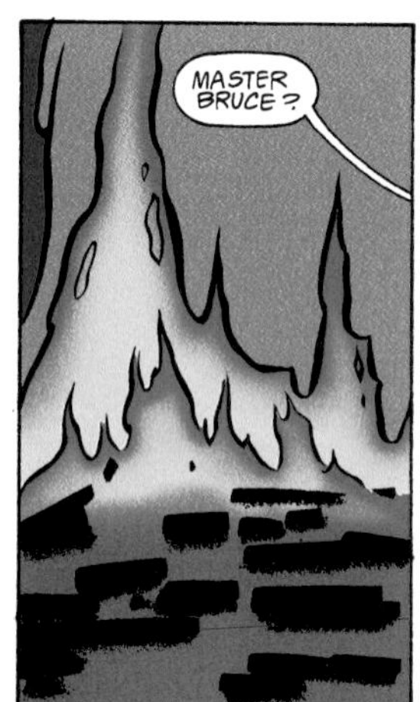
MASTER BRUCE?

MASTER BRUCE?
MASTER BRUCE?
HMM? OH... YES, ALFRED?
YOUR TEA, SIR.
JUST LEAVE IT ON THE TABLE, ALFRED. THANK YOU.

IT'S A YEAR TODAY, SIR.
A YEAR? A YEAR SINCE WHAT?
SINCE MASTER DICK WENT OFF ON HIS... HIS JOURNEY.

Oh, IS IT? I HADN'T NOTICED.

"OF COURSE YOU HADN'T, SIR."
THE END

CHAPTER 4: AS THE TWIG IS BENT

NIGHTWING

NIGHTWING

"AS THE TWIG IS BENT"

HILARY BADER writer
BO HAMPTON penciller
TERRY BEATTY inker
LEE LOUGHRIDGE colorist
TIM HARKINS letterer
DARREN VINCENZO and
SCOTT PETERSON editors

BATMAN CREATED BY BOB KANE

THEY... THEY CAN'T HEAR ME!

"LOOK OUT!"

I BETTER GO HELP--
KA-BOOM!
AHHHH!

oh NO!
BATMAN... ROBIN...
THEY MUST BE--

...CAUGHT!

YES! YES! YES! NOBODY GETS AWAY FROM US!

TAKE THAT, JOKER.
BATMAN, ROBIN AND TIM DRAKE ARE HERE TO FOIL YOUR DASTARDLY DOINGS!

THE THRILLING THREESOME! WHAT A TEAM. WHAT A GROUP. WHAT A---
OUCH!

Oh, MAN. MY DAD IS NEVER IN A MILLION YEARS GONNA BELIEVE THIS ONE.

YOU MAY HAVE ME SURROUNDED, JOKER, TWO-FACE, PENGUIN, SCAREFACE.
BUT I'VE GOT SOMETHING ON MY SIDE THAT YOU'LL NEVER HAVE...

...JUSTICE!
THWOK
SMACK
THOK
I TOLD YOU TO STOP WASTING YOUR TIME ON THIS MALARKEY.

YOU'VE GOT MORE IMPORTANT THINGS TO LEARN.
AND I DON'T WANT YOU DISRESPECTING TWO-FACE. HE'S A FRIEND OF THIS FAMILY. PUTS FOOD ON *YOUR* TABLE.
YOU BETTER GET THIS BAT GARBAGE OUT OF YOUR SYSTEM SOON. YOU AIN'T A KID ANYMORE...

YOU'RE GONNA HAVE TO LEARN TO BE USEFUL.
THAT'S WHAT I'M PLANNING ON, DAD.

COME ON, GEEK. GIVE US YOUR MONEY.
TEAR HIM APART UNTIL HE COUGHS SOMETHING UP.
UNHAND HIM.

YOU GOTTA BE KIDDIN', KID. NOBODY IN REAL LIFE SAYS "UNHAND."
LET HIM GO.
OR WHAT ?
COME ON DOWN HERE AND SAY THAT.
BEFORE I "UNSLICE" THE GEEK.

OW! YA LITTLE PUNK!
YOU'RE DEAD MEAT!

OOOF!
UNGH!

THAT WAS A WARNING. DID YOU UNDERSTAND IT?
YA, I DOT IT. YEAH. NOW DET OTH NY NECK.
MAGIC WORD?
PTHLEEZH!

... SO I MAY BE GONE A COUPLA DAYS.

YOU'RE DOIN' A JOB FOR TWO-FACE AGAIN.

I DON'T LIKE THE WAY YOU SAY HIS NAME. LIKE YOU AIN'T GOT NO RESPECT FOR HIM.

BLAMMO PUFFS

PANT
PANT PANT
WHEEZE

SORRY TIMMY-
THE HEATS ON-
I GOT TO LEAVE
FOR A WHILE-
HANG ON TO THESE
FOR ME-
DAD

YOU'LL BE OKAY, KID. YOU GOT SOMETHING SPECIAL. SOMETHING I NEVER HAD.

SLAM!
hmm?
DAD?

FOWLER'S MARKET
TODAY
WUNDER
BREAD

MILK

PANY PICNIC
FRIED CHICKEN
I'LL BET YOU'RE JOE MORRISEY'S SON. YOU LOOK JUST LIKE HIM.
uh... YEAH. THAT'S RIGHT.

SAMPLE OF OUR NEW SHAMPOO?
YEAH, SURE.

RASCHES
HEY! YOU CAN'T DO THAT!
THIS OUGHTA DO ME FOR A MONTH.

WHEEZ. COUGH.
COME BACK WITH MY DONUTS!

HA! NOW I GOTCHA.
UNGH!

IN YOUR DREAMS.
HUH?

AH!
JUST WAIT 'TIL I GET MY HANDS ON YOU, YOU LITTLE PUNK.

KID'S JUST ASKING FOR TROUBLE. AND IF HE DON'T FIND IT, I GOT A FEELING IT'LL FIND HIM.

HE SHOULDN'T BE EATING THIS GARBAGE ANYWAY.

HEY!
WHERE'S YOUR OLD MAN?

Eclaire
HEY!

MISSED ME, CHUMPS.

EAT MY DUST--
--UNGH!
GOING SOMEWHERE, KID?

SO, YOU'RE SHIFTY DRAKE'S BOY, huh ?
I'M NOT AFRAID OF YOU.
THEN YOU'RE DUMBER THAN YOUR OLD MAN.

"SORRY TIMMY. THE HEAT'S ON.
CLINK!

"I GOT TO LEAVE TOWN FOR AWHILE. HANG ON TO THIS FOR ME."

THAT SCROUNGY LITTLE TWO-BIT TWO-TIMER.
WHAT ABOUT THE KID ?
KILL HIM!
NO!
SORRY TIMMY. THE HEAT

OW!
AUGH!

GET HIM!
BEHIND YOU!
UNGH!
PING
PING
PING

OUTTA MY WAY!
OOOF!

oh, NO!

BATMAN, WE'RE GONNA --

UNGH!

BATMAN! WAKE UP!
WE'RE SITTING DUCKS HERE!
BEEP!

WHOA...
WHHHOOOOOSH!

THERE HE IS!
COME ON! HOW DO YOU START THIS STUPID THING?
AUTOPILOT. HOME.
COOL.

uh oh...

HELLO? WE'VE GOT A PROBLEM.

OMIGOD. OMIGOD. OMIGOD.

WHOOOOOAAA!

WHERE ARE YOU TAKING US?

YOU'RE HOME EARLY TONIGHT, SIR. DINNER WON'T BE READY UNTIL--

WHOA, IT'S THE ORIGINAL ROBIN SUIT, ISN'T IT ?
WHAT HAPPENED TO HIM ?
ALFRED ?
RIGHT HERE, SIR.

THE BOY... ?
HE'S HERE TOO, I'M AFRAID.
AT LEAST HE WAS.

BRUCE WAYNE, huh ?
PRESENTATION TO BRUCE WAYNE IN APPRECIATION
CHILDREN'S HOSPITAL
THANK YOU MR. WAYNE

SORRY YOU SAW THAT.

WHAT'S THE MATTER?

527-HA76

THEY FOUND A "*JOHN DOE*" IN METROPOLIS RIVER WHOSE PRINTS MATCH HIS FATHER'S.

SO HE'S NOT COMING BACK.

HE WAS NEVER GONNA, ANYWAY. HE WAS TOO SCARED.

OF WHAT? WHAT DID HE TAKE FROM TWO-FACE? WHY DID HE HIDE IT?

EXCUSE ME, SIR...

BUT THERE IS SOMETHING ON TELEVISION YOU MIGHT FIND ENLIGHTENING.

WHEN THESE TWO LIQUIDS ARE MIXED TOGETHER, THEY CREATE A NASTY GAS.

UNLESS I RECEIVE TWENTY-TWO MILLION DOLLARS...

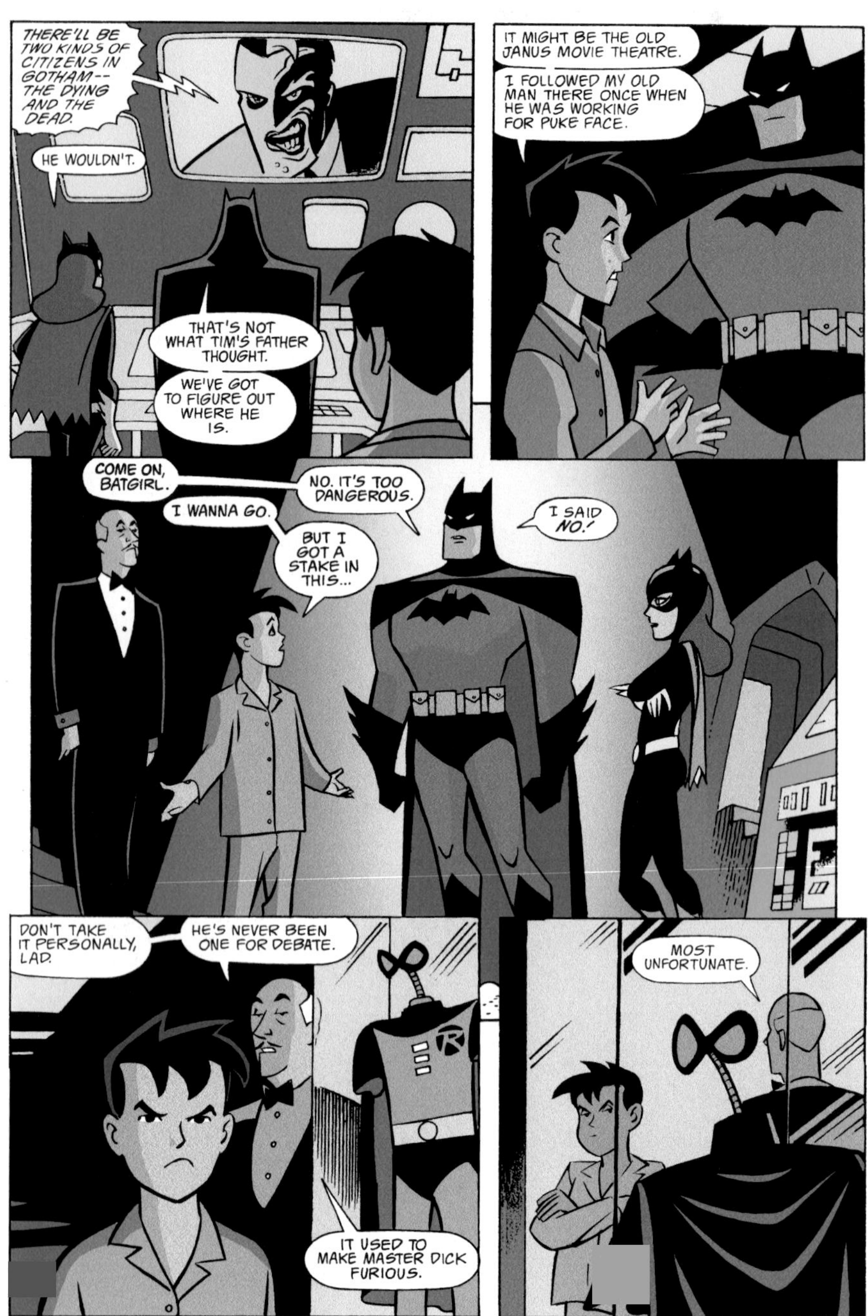
THERE'LL BE TWO KINDS OF CITIZENS IN GOTHAM-- THE DYING AND THE DEAD.
HE WOULDN'T.
THAT'S NOT WHAT TIM'S FATHER THOUGHT.
WE'VE GOT TO FIGURE OUT WHERE HE IS.
IT MIGHT BE THE OLD JANUS MOVIE THEATRE.
I FOLLOWED MY OLD MAN THERE ONCE WHEN HE WAS WORKING FOR PUKE FACE.
COME ON, BATGIRL.
NO. IT'S TOO DANGEROUS.
I WANNA GO.
BUT I GOT A STAKE IN THIS...
I SAID NO.!
DON'T TAKE IT PERSONALLY, LAD.
HE'S NEVER BEEN ONE FOR DEBATE.
IT USED TO MAKE MASTER DICK FURIOUS.
MOST UNFORTUNATE.

GET THE MASKS, BOYS. THEY'VE HAD THEIR TWO-MINUTE WARNING.
THUDD!
WHAT WAS THAT?
EXIT
HE'S HERE.
REELS #516-A

SO... "IT USED TO MAKE MASTER DICK FURIOUS" huh?

OOOF.
UNGH!
PROPS

WELL, I'M NOT MASTER DICK!
JANUS
CLOSED

OOOF
THWACK
SMACK
UNGH!
AUGH!
I HOPE I HAVEN'T MISSED ALL THE FUN.

TWO-FACE HAS SET THE TIMER. WE HAVE TO STOP IT BEFORE THE CHEMICALS--
YOU'RE TOO LATE, BATMAN.
OOOPS.
OOOF!
EXCUSE ME.
L-15
PROPS

Oh, NO.
EXIT
REELS 2-14
LOT 2-14

IT'S YOUR KIND OF SHOW, PUKE FACE -- A DOUBLE FEATURE.
OUWCH. YEOW!

OOF!
Ha! BEEN A LONG TIME, BIRD-BOY.

LET THE KID GO, TWO-FACE.
MAKE ONE MOVE AND I'LL WRING HIS FEATHERED LITTLE NECK.

NOT THAT IT'S GONNA MATTER IN ABOUT TEN SECONDS.

PLENTY OF TIME.

OOOF!

UNGH!

THE BATARANG, TOO.
BUT... ALL RIGHT.
I DON'T WANT YOU WEARING IT AGAIN...

UNTIL YOU'VE EARNED IT.
EARNED IT ?
WE BEGIN TOMORROW. FIVE O'CLOCK.
IN THE MORNING ?

CROOKS DON'T KEEP BANKER'S HOURS.
I'LL BE READY.

THE BATARANG ?
I BELIEVE MASTER TIM HAS NEED OF IT.
NEED ? WHY WOULD HE NEED THE BATARANG ?

"NOT FOR WHAT YOU MIGHT SUPPOSE, MASTER BRUCE."
THE END

CHAPTER 5: YOU CAN'T GO HOME AGAIN

NIGHTWING

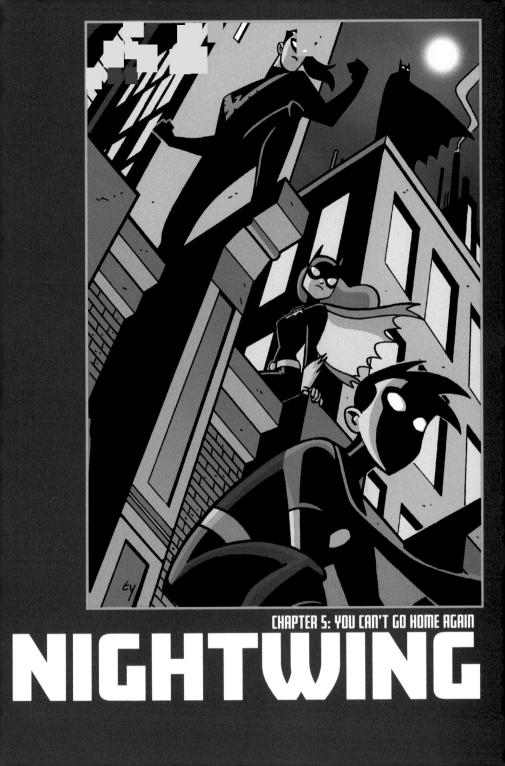

NIGHTWING

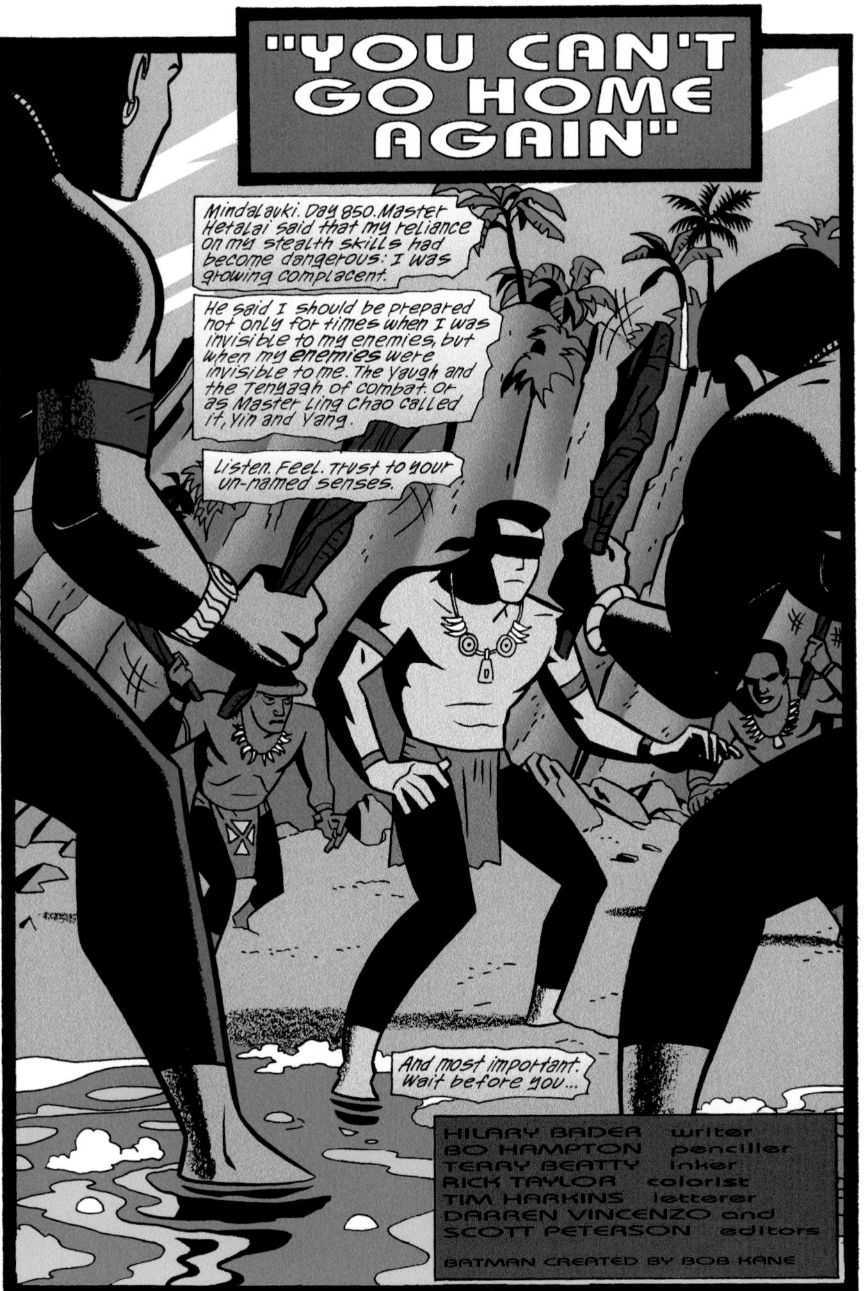
"YOU CAN'T GO HOME AGAIN"
Mindalauki. Day 850. Master Hetalai said that my reliance on my stealth skills had become dangerous: I was growing complacent.
He said I should be prepared not only for times when I was invisible to my enemies, but when my enemies were invisible to me. The Yaugh and the Tenyagh of combat. Or as Master Ling Chao called it, Yin and Yang.
Listen. Feel. Trust to your un-named senses.
And most important. Wait before you...
HILARY BADER writer
BO HAMPTON penciller
TERRY BEATTY inker
RICK TAYLOR colorist
TIM HARKINS letterer
DARREN VINCENZO and
SCOTT PETERSON editors
BATMAN CREATED BY BOB KANE

...move!
UNGH!
WHACK
CLOSE.

TWO IN FRONT.
AHH!
WHOA!

THAT SHOULD TAKE CARE OF--UNGH!
HAH!

"HAH" YOURSELF, KUMAKIT!
OOOF.
AGH!

ENOUGH!

YOU HAVE SHARPENED YOUR BATTLE SENSES WELL, JAOHAHN.
BUT SHARPENED SENSES ARE FOR MORE THAN JUST COMBAT. THERE IS A WHOLE OTHER PART OF LIFE. YOU MUST LEARN THAT.

BUT I HAVE NOTHING MORE TO TEACH YOU.
THEN I WILL BE GOING.
YOUR THIRST FOR KNOWLEDGE IS OVERSHADOWING ALL OTHER ELEMENTS. YOUR LIFE IS WITHOUT BALANCE.
AND ANY LIFE WITHOUT BALANCE IS LIKE A VOLCANO. THE PRESSURE WILL BUILD...

...UNTIL IT EXPLODES.
I DO WHAT I MUST.
WHAT WILL YOU LEARN NOW?
WHEN I WAS IN TIBET I HEARD OF A CULT OF MYSTICS IN THE HIMALAYAS WHO, IT IS SAID, HAVE MASTERED THE SECRET OF FLIGHT.

"YOU MAY LEARN TO FLY. BUT DO NOT FORGET THEN HOW TO WALK."
I WILL FORGET NOTHING YOU HAVE TOLD ME, MASTER.

SIR! SIR! YOUR HOLINESS? MASTER?
NOTHING SO GRAND. I AM MERELY A NOVITIATE.
COME. WALK WITH ME.
I HAVE HEARD OF A GROUP OF MONKS WHO LIVE HIDDEN IN THE MOUNTAIN TOP.
AND YOU WISH TO FIND THEM SO THEY CAN TEACH YOU THE SECRET OF FLIGHT.
YOU ARE NOT THE FIRST TO SEARCH FOR THEM. BUT YOU WILL HAVE A HARD TIME FINDING A GUIDE.
WHY?
BECAUSE EVERY ABLE-BODIED SHERPA AND HIS BROTHER HAS BEEN HIRED ON BY *THEM*.
WHO ARE THEY?
MEN WHO SEARCH, AS YOU DO, FOR THE "*HERMITS OF THE MOUNTAIN.*"
THEN IF I FOLLOW THEM, I WILL FIND WHAT I AM LOOKING FOR.
WHAT YOU ARE LOOKING FOR WILL NOT BE FOUND OUTSIDE YOU. BUT, YES THEY WILL LEAD YOU TO THE "*HERMITS.*"
THANK YOU. YOU HAVE BEEN A GREAT HELP TO ME.
I LIVE TO SERVE. AS DO YOU.

WHAT'S THE PROBLEM ?
LOOK. WE HIRED YOU TO LEAD US TO THE MOUNTAIN. IF YOU CAN'T HANDLE IT...
WHY YOU CARRY SO MUCH WASTE ?
I HANDLE. NEED TO HIRE MORE BEARERS.
THEN DO IT. I'VE TOLD YOU. FOR MY EMPLOYER, MONEY IS NO OBJECT.
QUESTION NOT MONEY.
EVERYTHING IS A QUESTION OF MONEY.
DONUTS
EXCUSE ME, SIR ? I OVERHEAD WHAT YOU WERE SAYING.
YES.
I'D LIKE TO HIRE ON.
SKINNY LITTLE WESTERNER. YOU NOT LAST THE MORNING.
I CAN PULL MY OWN WEIGHT.
HM. WHAT YOU WANT GO UP MOUNTAIN FOR ?
THAT'S MY BUSINESS.
OKAY, WESTERN BOY. BUT YOU SLOW US DOWN, WE LEAVE YOU BEHIND.

YOU DO OKAY, WESTERN BOY. BUT THIS ONLY FIRST WEEK. YOU GONNA LAST?

THIS IS A WALK IN THE PARK.
DON'T THINK PARK THIS STEEP.
HAHA HA
YOU GOT THE ENERGY TO LAUGH...

THAT MEANS YOU GOT THE ENERGY TO GO FASTER.
NO. WE REST THE NIGHT.
THIS AIN'T A PLEASURE TRIP. WE GOT A SCHEDULE TO KEEP.
YOU WANT FIND MONASTERY. WE TAKE. BUT NO RUSH.

WHY DO THEY WANT TO FIND THE "HERMIT MONKS"?
THEY HIRE. I GUIDE. NO ASK QUESTIONS.
MAYBE YOU SHOULD.

WESTERN BOY TOO CURIOUS. CARRY, WALK, REST. THAT IS ENOUGH TO DO.
MAYBE. BUT I'M GETTING A BAD FEELING ABOUT THESE GUYS.

HOW DO WE EVEN KNOW THESE MONKS HAVE THIS "SPIRIT OF THE ETERNAL" SOMETHING-OR-OTHER.
WE'VE BEEN HIRED TO STEAL IT, NOT ASK QUESTIONS ABOUT IT.
STILL. DON'T YOU EVER WONDER WHY HE WANTS IT?

I MEAN, IT MUST HOLD SOME INCREDIBLE POWER IF HE'S WILLING TO FOOT THE BILL FOR THIS WHOLE EXPEDITION.
IF YOU KNOW WHAT'S GOOD FOR YOU, YOU'LL JUST DO WHAT YOU'RE TOLD. QUESTIONING RA'S AL GHUL'S MOTIVE'S AIN'T THE HEALTHIEST PASTIME.

RA'S AL GHUL?
AND NEITHER IS FAILING HIM. WE FIND THE MONASTERY OF THESE MONKS, WE TAKE THE STATUE, AND WE'RE GONE.
NO LOOTING. NO STICKY FINGERS. UNDERSTOOD?

YOU'RE NOT AS QUIET AS YOU THINK YOU ARE.
YOU NOT AS CLEVER AS YOU THINK YOU ARE.

A HUNGRY PORTER CANNOT CARRY.
THAT'S NOT IMPORTANT NOW. THESE MEN WE CARRY FOR WORK FOR SOMEONE I KNOW. A VERY EVIL MAN.
HUNGER IS ALWAYS IMPORTANT. COME. EAT. WE WILL TALK TOMORROW.

NOW, WESTERN BOY. WHAT YOU THINK SO IMPORTANT.
THE MAN THESE PEOPLE WORK FOR IS A VERY POWERFUL MAN.
HE HAS SENT THEM TO STEAL SOMETHING FROM THE MONKS.
YOU HEAR THIS?
YES. AND I KNOW THIS MAN. IF THE MONKS HAVE ANYTHING OF POWER, HE WILL FIND A WAY TO USE IT FOR EVIL.
THEN WE WILL NOT LET THEM STEAL IT.
WHOOSSH
KKRRRAACKK!
WAIT.
WHAT ARE YOU DOING? GET UP! GET MOVING.
SNOW IS SOFT. TOO SOFT.
SNIFF
SMELL. WARMTH. TOO DANGEROUS. WE MUST TURN BACK.
WE PAID YOU TO GUIDE US TO THE MONASTERY AND YOU WILL.
DANGER OF AVALANCHE TOO GREAT. ANOTHER TIME.

NO. NOW!
YOU SHOOT THAT OFF AND A MOUNTAIN OF SNOW WILL COME CRASHING DOWN.
I DIDN'T ASK YOU FOR ADVICE.

HUNGH!
HEY!
NOW SHUT UP. AND THE REST OF YOU GO MOVE.
OR THE OLD MAN GETS IT.
HE WAS RIGHT. YOU ARE EVIL MEN. WE WILL NOT SERVE YOU ANY LONGER.

YOU'LL DO WHAT I SAY--

HE'LL DO WHAT HE WANTS!
OOOF!

GET AWAY FROM HERE. FAST.
WHAT ABOUT YOU, WESTERN BOY?
I'LL BE ALL--

ANGH!
GO!

UNGH!

THAT SHOULD TAKE CARE OF HIM.
HOW'RE WE GOING TO FIND THE STATUE WITHOUT THE SHERPAS? AND WHERE'S SLY?
I FOUND IT! I FOUND IT!

THERE'S A PATH. IT LEADS TO THE MONASTERY.
WHAT'LL WE DO WITH HIM?
BURY HIM!

HERE WE GO, PRETTY BOY.
ELEVATOR GOING DOWN.
HANG ON, GRAYSON. KEEP CONTROL. EVERYTHING RELAXED AND YOU'LL BE ALL RIGHT.
LIKE MASTER HETALAI TAUGHT YOU. AND MASTER CHIN. AND MASTER VOLDDONI. AND MASTER LING CHAO. DO NOT FIGHT IT. GO WITH IT.
DARN GOOD THING I'M NOT AFRAID OF FALL--
WHA!
UNGH!
PLEASANT DREAMS.
HOW ABOUT A NICE BLANKET... OF SNOW!

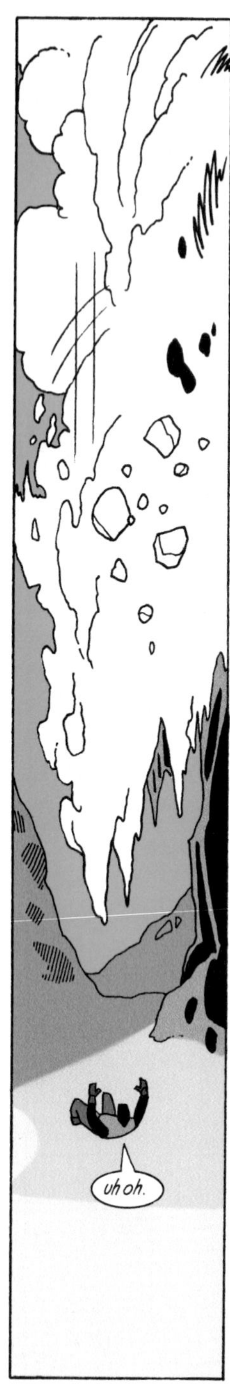
uh oh.

BREATHE, GRAYSON. BREATHE AND THINK. THERE'S GOT TO BE A WAY OUT OF THIS.
AND WHATEVER YOU DO, DON'T FALL ASLEEP.

THAT OUGHTTA KEEP HIM SNUG.
NOW WHERE'S THAT MOUNTAIN PASS?

SCRATCH... SCRATCH
HM?

Whoa!

YES. BREATHE DEEPLY.
GASP
THE AIR WAS DISAPPEARING.
YOU WERE UNDER FOR A VERY LONG TIME. BUT YOU WILL BE ALL RIGHT.

THE MEN WHO WERE WITH ME --
GONE.
THEY WERE LOOKING FOR THE MONASTERY.
AND THEY FOUND IT.

THEY TOOK AWAY A GREAT AND POWERFUL TREASURE. YOU MUST GET IT BACK FOR US.
US? YOU ARE ONE OF THEM? THE HERMITS?
THE FLYING MONKS?

WE ARE SOMETIMES CALLED THAT.
I WAS SEARCHING FOR YOU. I WANTED...
WE KNOW WHAT YOU WANTED. BUT WE WANT SOMETHING FROM YOU.

WHY DO YOU NEED ME?
BECAUSE THEY HAVE TAKEN THE TREASURE TO THE WESTERN WORLD. YOUR WORLD. A PLACE WE CANNOT GO.

HOW WILL WE GET BACK UP? WE HAVE NO CLIMBING EQUIPMENT.
WE WILL GO *DOWN!*
DOWN? HOW?
FLY!

WHOOOAAA!

THAT WAS THE BEST RIDE OF MY LIFE.
LET'S DO IT AGAIN.
I HAVE FORSAKEN THE WORLD OF WESTERN MEN. I CAN GO NO FURTHER.
BUT *YOU* MUST. HERE!
WHAT'S THIS?
A TRADE. OUR SECRET OF "FLIGHT" FOR THE STATUE.
FIND THE STATUE AND RETURN IT TO US, BEFORE IT FALLS INTO THE EVIL ONES' HANDS.
IT'S AS GOOD AS FOUND.
NOT BAD. NEEDS SOMETHING, THOUGH.
THERE. NOW I'M READY TO FACE *GOTHAM.*

BEAUTIFUL, ISN'T SHE?
WHO WOULD IMAGINE THE KIND OF POWER SHE POSSESSES?
THE SPIRIT OF THE ETERNAL SOUL.

SHAPED AND FORGED BY CHEMICALS FROM THE LAZARUS PIT ITSELF.
WHY, IT WAS PRACTICALLY ORDAINED THAT IT SHOULD BE MINE.
WITH THIS, I CAN STAVE OFF MY NEED FOR RENEWAL FOR DECADES. ACCESS TO THE POWER OF THE LAZARUS PIT WILL BE IN MY HANDS.
THUD!

CHECK THAT OUT. CAREFULLY.
THERE ARE MEN IN GOTHAM WITH WHOM I WOULD RATHER NOT HAVE TO TANGLE.
NO ONE IN HERE, BOSS.

"NO ONE." NOW THERE'S A NAME I HAVEN'T CONSIDERED USING.

BUT I WAS THINKING MORE ALONG THE LINES OF...
... NIGHTSTALKER?
OOOF!
UNGH!
WHO'S THERE?
SHOW YOUR--
UNGH!
I'LL BE TAKING THAT NOW.
I THINK NOT.
NOW LET GO OF HER.
NO!

I DON'T KNOW WHO YOU ARE--
AND I'M GOING TO KEEP IT THAT WAY.
YOU EXPEND A LOT OF ENERGY WITH SMART REMARKS, YOUNG MAN.

IF I WERE YOU, I'D SAVE IT FOR MORE IMPORTANT THINGS.
UNGH!
BUT YOU'RE NOT ME.
HOW LONG DO YOU THINK YOU CAN HOLD AGAINST ME, CHILD?

DO YOU KNOW WHO I AM?
I AM LIFE. I AM HISTORY. I AM TIME ITSELF.
YEAH, WELL, I'M A FEW THINGS MYSELF.

SOON, ONE OF THE THINGS YOU'LL BE IS: DEAD!
WHAOOOAA!

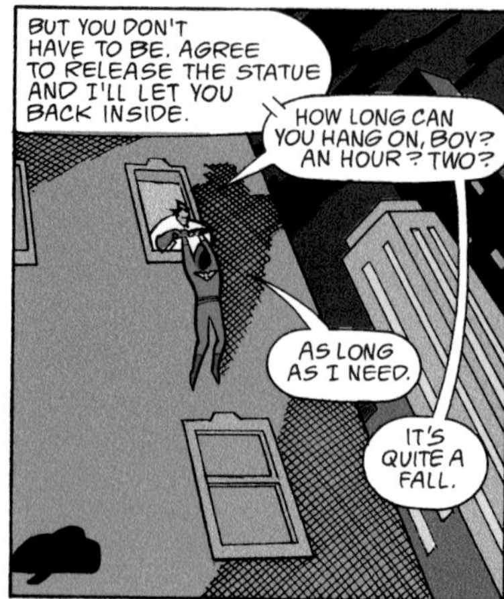
BUT YOU DON'T HAVE TO BE. AGREE TO RELEASE THE STATUE AND I'LL LET YOU BACK INSIDE.
HOW LONG CAN YOU HANG ON, BOY? AN HOUR? TWO?
AS LONG AS I NEED.
IT'S QUITE A FALL.

ANGH!
GOOD THING I'M NOT AFRAID OF HEIGHTS.

YOU FOOLISH BOY.
AFTER THEY SCRAPE YOU FROM THE SIDEWALK, THE STATUE WILL STILL BE MINE.
NOT READY TO BE SIDEWALK STROGANOFF JUST YET, RA'S.
A CHILD. TRICKED BY A CHILD.
BUT TIME IS ON MY SIDE, BOY. I HAVE MORE THAN YOU CAN IMAGINE.
I WILL HAVE THE STATUE BACK. SOME-DAY.
WELL, THAT WAS A CLOSE ONE, BUT YOU'RE SAFE NOW. SOON YOU'LL BE WHERE YOU BELONG.
YOU NEED TO GO HOME.
AND MAYBE...

"...SO DO I."
YOU WORK WITH ME, TIM, YOU FOLLOW THE RULES.
RULE NUMBER ONE...
...YOU GIVE ME EVERYTHING YOU'VE GOT.
RULE NUMBER TWO...
...THEN YOU GIVE ME MORE.
AND RULE NUMBER THREE.
OOF!
I MAKE THE RULES.
WATCH OUT FOR THAT LAST ONE, KID...
IT'S A KILLER.
DICK?
MY WORD... HOW YOU'VE CHANGED!
HEY, NO ONE CAN BE A BOY WONDER FOREVER.

YOU'VE CHANGED.
SO HAVE YOU. MISS ME ?
DON'T *EVEN* GO THERE.

I'M SORRY TO INTERRUPT THE REUNION, BUT THE BATSIGNAL --
IT'S ALL RIGHT, ALFRED. WORK ALWAYS COMES FIRST.
DOESN'T IT ?
YES.

I... I SUPPOSE YOU'LL BE WANTING THIS.
NO THANKS, KID. I BROUGHT MY OWN.

SO IF YOU'RE NOT "*ROBIN*" ANYMORE, WHAT DO WE CALL YOU ?
CALL ME...

...NIGHTWING.
HB BH TB LL '97
THE END

CHAPTER 6: WITH A PRICE ON HIS HEAD!

NIGHTWING

NIGHTWING

WITH A PRICE ON HIS HEAD!
YEEHAH!
YEEEEEEHAH!
TY TEMPLETON WRITER
RICK BURCHETT PENCILLER
TERRY BEATTY INKER
LEE LOUGHRIDGE COLORIST
TIM HARKINS LETTERER
DARREN VINCENZO EDITOR

DRAT! YOU'RE STILL COMING AFTER ME?
WHAT IS IT WITH YOU? DO I OWE YOU MONEY?
HEADS UP!
I'M SHOOTING MY MOUTH OFF AGAIN.
HA HA HA HAHA
BLAM!
KA-BOOOM!
ROBIN! STREET LEVEL DAMAGE CONTROL! GO!
AYE AYE, CAPTAIN!

EEEEEEEE
YOU'LL HAVE TO KEEP THIS OUR SECRET...
BATMAN SAYS I'M TOO YOUNG TO PICK UP GIRLS.
WE'VE JUST RECEIVED WORD THAT BATMAN AND THE JOKER HAVE BEEN SIGHTED IN GOTHAM SQUARE...
REID
ASTOR
CAMERA CREWS ARE ON THEIR WAY, AND WE'LL CUT AWAY THERE AS SOON AS WE'RE READY.
IN THE MEANTIME, WE'RE ABOUT TO GO TO THE BOARDROOM OF REID PHARMACEUTICALS, WHERE PRESIDENT AND CEO G. DOUGLAS REID HAS CALLED A SUDDEN AND MYSTERIOUS PRESS CONFERENCE.

REID HAS LONG BEEN A NEWSMAKER IN GOTHAM CITY...
SINCE HIS UNSUCCESSFUL BID FOR MAYOR EIGHT YEARS AGO.--
--HE HAS STAYED IN THE NEWS WITH HIS SPECTACULAR DONATIONS TO LOCAL HOSPITALS AND CLINICS.
BUT THESE DAYS THE NEWS HAS BEEN TRAGIC FOR THE REID FAMILY.
HE IS PICTURED HERE WITH HIS SON, GLENN, IN A PHOTO TAKEN ONE WEEK AGO--
--JUST TWO DAYS BEFORE GLENN BECAME THE LATEST VICTIM IN THE JOKER'S RECENT CRIME SPREE.
HE HAD IT COMING!
HE SPLASHED MUD ON MY NEW KHAKI WALKING SHORTS.

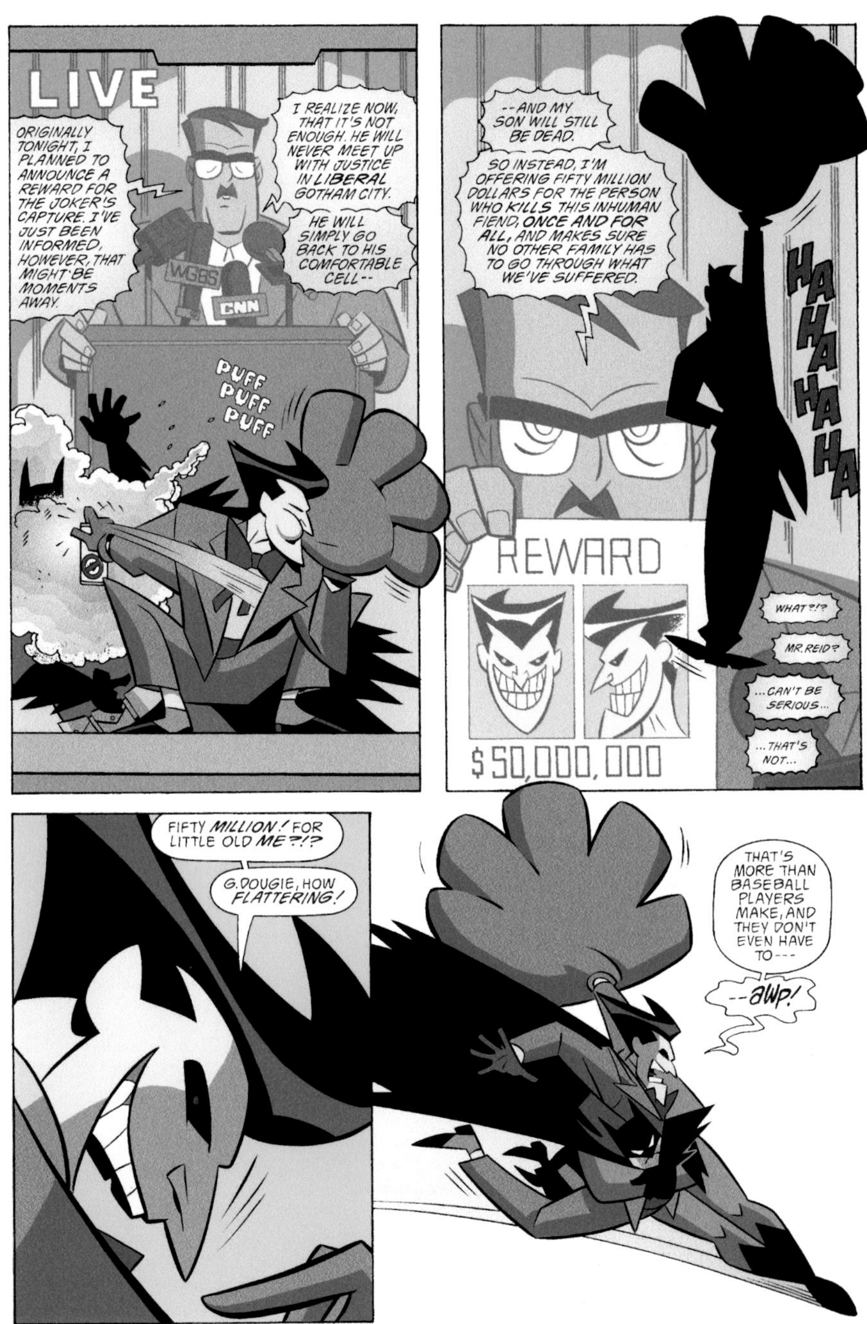
LIVE
ORIGINALLY TONIGHT, I PLANNED TO ANNOUNCE A REWARD FOR THE JOKER'S CAPTURE. I'VE JUST BEEN INFORMED, HOWEVER, THAT MIGHT BE MOMENTS AWAY.
I REALIZE NOW, THAT IT'S NOT ENOUGH. HE WILL NEVER MEET UP WITH JUSTICE IN LIBERAL GOTHAM CITY.
HE WILL SIMPLY GO BACK TO HIS COMFORTABLE CELL--
WGBS
CNN
PUFF
PUFF
PUFF
--AND MY SON WILL STILL BE DEAD.
SO INSTEAD, I'M OFFERING FIFTY MILLION DOLLARS FOR THE PERSON WHO KILLS THIS INHUMAN FIEND, ONCE AND FOR ALL, AND MAKES SURE NO OTHER FAMILY HAS TO GO THROUGH WHAT WE'VE SUFFERED.
HAHAHAHAHA
REWARD
$50,000,000
WHAT?!?
MR. REID?
...CAN'T BE SERIOUS...
...THAT'S NOT...
FIFTY MILLION! FOR LITTLE OLD ME?!?
G. DOUGIE, HOW FLATTERING!
THAT'S MORE THAN BASEBALL PLAYERS MAKE, AND THEY DON'T EVEN HAVE TO---
--awp!

YOU IDIOT! CAN'T YOU SEE THIS IS A ONE-MAN GLOVE? IT WON'T HOLD OUR WEIGHT!

FWOOSH

"WE'LL BE COMING BACK TO THE REMARKABLE DEVELOPMENTS AT THE REID CORPORATION IN MOMENTS. BUT WE CUT AWAY LIVE NOW--"

"--AS CAMERA CREWS ARE ON THE SCENE OF GOTHAM SQUARE--"

GORDON, IT'S DR. SPELLING, OVER AT ARKHAM.
I SAW THE NEWS EARLIER TONIGHT... ABOUT THE JOKER...
WELL, I'M AFRAID WE HAVE A SITUATION BREWING HERE.
IT'S PROBABLY BEST IF YOU DON'T TRANSFER THE JOKER BACK TO ARKHAM TONIGHT.
WHAT KIND OF 'SITUATION'?
NOT ANOTHER ESCAPE, I HOPE...
HEAVENS, NO! NOTHING SINCE THE RIDDLER LAST MONTH.
I DON'T KNOW QUITE HOW TO SAY THIS...

FOR THAT KIND OF MONEY, I TRUST NO ONE.
HEE HEE
THERE'S NOWHERE YOU'D BE SAFE...
HEE HEE...
... SO I'M KEEPING YOU WITH ME UNTIL THIS GETS SORTED OUT.
WE'RE MOVING *IN* TOGETHER ?!?
THAT'S A BIG STEP. I'M NOT SURE WE'RE READY.
BUT, **WOW-WOWW-WEEE!** NICE CRIB, BUNKIE!
I'M NOT CLEANING UP AFTER THE BATS, THOUGH. I HAVE TO DRAW THE LINE *SOMEWHERE*.
DO I GET TO WATCH TV?
WHAT YOU *GET*--

--IS TO BE HANDCUFFED TO THE RAILING UNTIL I CAN FIND A BETTER PLACE TO PUT YOU.
AWP!
KLANGK

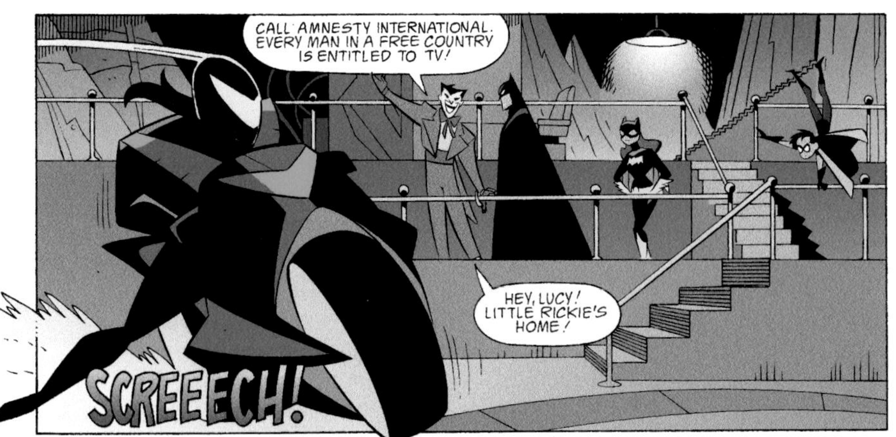
CALL AMNESTY INTERNATIONAL. EVERY MAN IN A FREE COUNTRY IS ENTITLED TO TV!
HEY, LUCY! LITTLE RICKIE'S HOME!
SCREEECH!

I SAW THE NEWS. I FIGURED YOU'D HAVE HIM HERE.
DO YOU HAVE ANY IDEA OF THE TIME, YOUNG MAN-- YOUR FATHER AND I HAVE BEEN WORRIED SICK!
NEED A HAND?
IT'S COMPLETELY UNDER CONTROL, NIGHTWING.

STEP!
STEP!
STEP!
MORE COMPANY? IT'S A PARTY!

STEP!
STEP!
STEP!

ROBIN!
I'M ON IT.

WHUFF!
MASTER TIM...? WHAT IN HEAVEN'S NAME ARE YOU--?
SHHH! CHILL! BATMAN'S GOT THE JOKER IN THERE.
YOU CAN'T BE RECOGNIZED AS BRUCE WAYNE'S BUTLER OR THE WHOLE JIG IS UP.
FOR THE NEXT FEW DAYS, YOU'LL HAVE TO TAKE A LOOK AT THE UPSTAIRS MONITORS BEFORE YOU COME DOWN, TO MAKE SURE IT'S SAFE.
I QUITE UNDERSTAND. IN THE MEANTIME--
WE'RE NEEDED.
GORDON'S LIT THE SIGNAL.

ROBIN, YOU'RE WITH ME.
NIGHTWING, YOU'RE WELCOME TO COME ALONG...
NO THANKS. I PATROL THE STREETS ON MY OWN NOW.
I'M LEAVING YOU TO WATCH THE JOKER. CAN YOU HANDLE IT?
NO SWEAT, BOSS.

I WON'T TAKE IT BACK. I MEANT WHAT I SAID, AND I DON'T CARE WHAT THE CONSEQUENCES ARE...
I'M GOING TO SEE JUSTICE DONE, AND I HAVE SOME OF THE BEST LEGAL MINDS IN THE COUNTRY TO KEEP ME FROM SEEING THE INSIDE OF A CELL...

I APPRECIATE WHAT YOU'RE GOING THROUGH, DOUGLAS, BUT YOU HAVE TO RETRACT THAT BOUNTY.
YOU SIMPLY CAN'T HIRE KILLERS OVER THE TELEVISION AIRWAVES...
BUT--
DOUGLAS, DON'T YOU HANG UP ON ME--

HE'S A GOOD MAN.
BUT IF THE JOKER DIES, I'LL HAVE TO HAVE HIM ARRESTED.
DON'T WORRY, YOU WON'T HAVE TO.

JOKER'S SAFE.
I ASSUMED HE WAS WITH YOU. THAT'S *ONE* WEIGHT OFF MY SHOULDERS AT LEAST.
BUT THAT'S NOT WHY I CALLED YOU HERE.
THIS LITTLE MINI RECORDER WAS DROPPED OFF AT THE FRONT DESK FIFTEEN MINUTES AGO.
HEY NOW, HO NOW, BAT-DOLT!

I'VE GOT A RIDDLE FOR YOU, IF YOU CAN TAKE DIRECTION, THAT IS...
"T" IS FOR THESPIAN, AND IF T'S WERE D'S THEN I'D BE AN OPPOSITE IN ONE WORD!
WHERE AM I?
THESPA-WHO? WHAT ON EARTH IS ALL THAT SUPPOSED TO MEAN?
I THINK I KNOW, ROBIN.
THESPIAN IS ANOTHER WORD FOR ACTOR.
"TAKE DIRECTION" IS ANOTHER THEATER REFERENCE.
THE RIDDLE WORD IS "UPTOWN."
IF T'S WERE D'S THEN THE WORD WOULD BE SPELLED "UPDOWN"...
... AND BE AN OPPOSITE IN ONE WORD.
THE UPTOWN THEATRE HAS BEEN ABANDONED FOR A FEW YEARS, BUT IT'S A SAFE BET HE'S UP TO SOMETHING IN THERE.

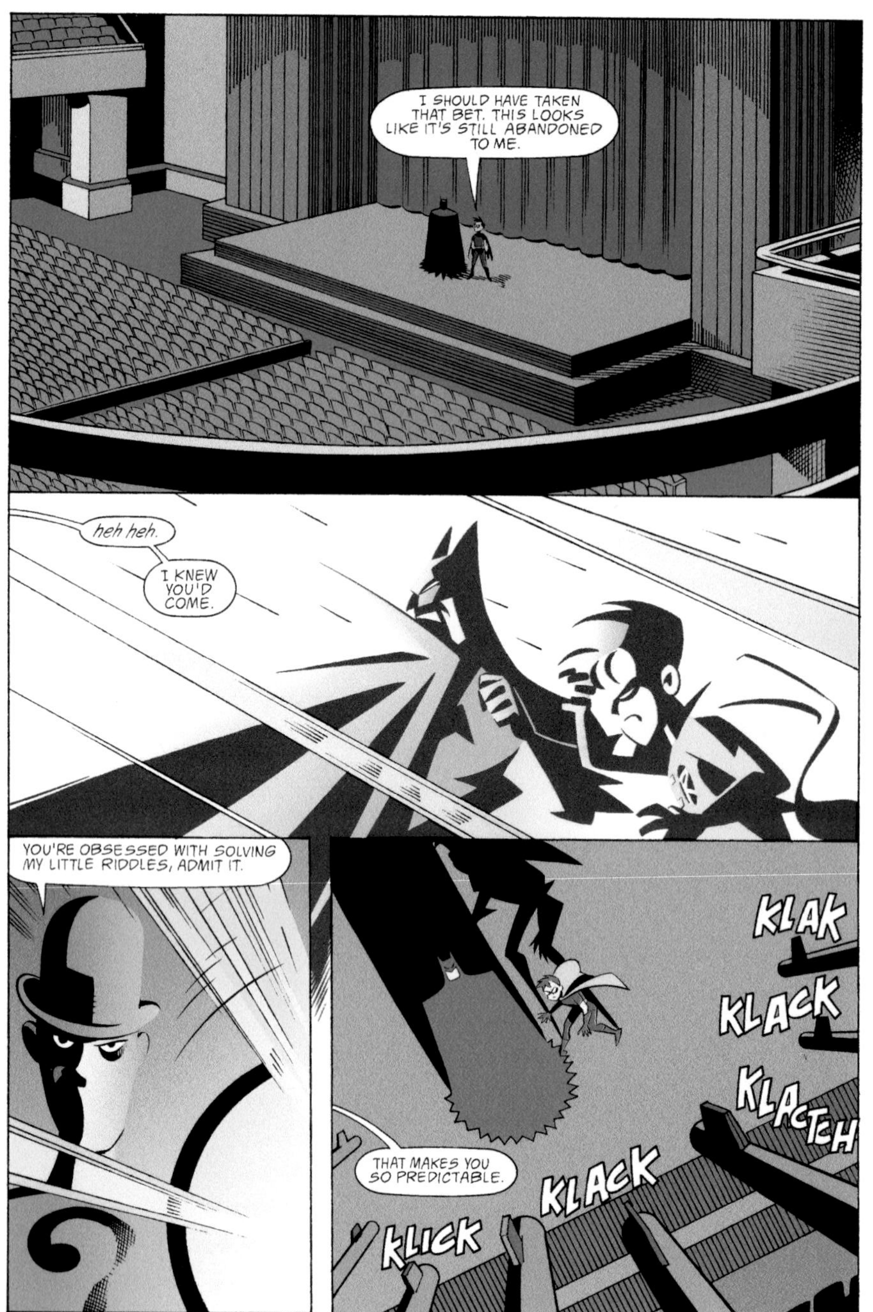
I SHOULD HAVE TAKEN THAT BET. THIS LOOKS LIKE IT'S STILL ABANDONED TO ME.
heh heh.
I KNEW YOU'D COME.
YOU'RE OBSESSED WITH SOLVING MY LITTLE RIDDLES, ADMIT IT.
KLAK
KLACK
KLACTCH
THAT MAKES YOU SO PREDICTABLE.
KLACK
KLICK

SO HERE'S THE DEAL...
I'M TAKING YOUNG ROBIN PRISONER AND YOU CAN HAVE HIM BACK FOR A TIDY RANSOM.
A NICE ROUND FEE... FIFTY MILLION DOLLARS.
OR MERCHANDISE WORTH AN EQUIVALENT AMOUNT.
I KNOW YOU HAVE THE JOKER, I SAW IT ON TV.
I'VE NEVER QUITE FORGIVEN THAT CLOWN FOR TRYING TO KILL ME A FEW YEARS BACK.
KILLING HIM WILL BE SUCH A LOVELY WAY TO EARN FIFTY MILLION BIG ONES.
WELL, ENOUGH CHITCHAT. TIME TO BAG ME A HOSTAGE.
C'MERE KID.

STAY WHERE YOU ARE, ROBIN.
OKEY DOKE, BUT YOU'RE NOT GOING TO LIKE PLAN B.
BETCHA THAT BRAT KNOWS WHERE JOKER IS, SAME AS YOU DO. NOW, I KNOW I'D NEVER GET THE INFORMATION OUT OF A TOUGH GUY LIKE YOU, BATS...
BUT THE BOY MIGHT NOT BE SO RESISTANT TO PHYSICAL PERSUASION.
oh YEAH?

IT'S A QUARTER TO THREE -- THERE'S NO ONE IN THE PLACE 'CEPT YOU AND ME--
WHATSAMATTER DON'T LIKE THE CLASSICS? SOMETHING MORE MODERN, THEN.
SHOULD I STAY OR SHOULD I GO NOW-- ?
Oh, LISTEN TO ME RAIL ON... YOU CAN'T GET A WORD IN EDGEWISE.
THIS ISN'T MUCH OF A SLUMBER PARTY IF WE DON'T START TELLING EACH OTHER OUR SECRETS.
I GOT IT! YOU TELL ME ABOUT THE FIRST GUY YOU EVER KISSED.
I'LL TELL YOU ABOUT THE FIRST ONE I EVER KILLED.
SHY ONE, AREN'T YOU?
YOU'RE A SICK ANIMAL, JOKER. I HAVE NOTHING TO SAY TO YOU.
I THINK SOMEONE'S GOT A CRUSH ON ME!
THAT'S ALL RIGHT. I'LL GO FIRST THEN.
WOULD YOU LIKE TO HEAR A SECRET I'D NEVER EVER TELL BATMAN? IT'S A REALLY JUICY ONE, TOO...
WHAT ARE Y...?

WAIT! WAIT!
THE WALLS HAVE EARS!

AND WINGS, FUR, AND TEETH FROM THE LOOKS OF THINGS.
ECCH! BATS EVERYWHERE. YOU PEOPLE ARE NUTS.

NEVER MIND.
ANYWAY, YOU REALLY HAVE TO PROMISE NOT TO TELL.

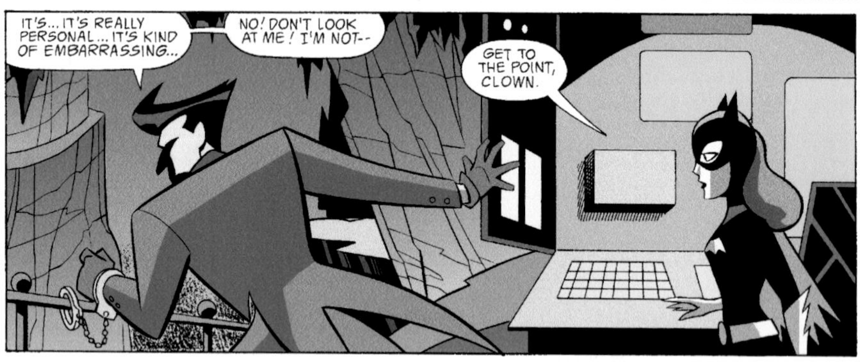
IT'S... IT'S REALLY PERSONAL... IT'S KIND OF EMBARRASSING...
NO! DON'T LOOK AT ME! I'M NOT--
GET TO THE POINT, CLOWN.

Sheesh! SUCH A GROUCH! OKAY, HERE'S THE GAG --
YOU SEE THESE HANDCUFFS?
I...

...COULD HAVE GOTTEN OUT OF THEM ANY TIME...

...I WANTED..
I JUST HAD TO WAIT UNTIL IT WAS FUNNY!
HA HA HA HA
HA HA HA

WHOOOPIE! HAND-TO-HAND COMBAT!
AND YOU'RE "UNARMED."
HAHAHAHAHA
SWOOSH!
DON'T WORRY. YOU'RE STILL GOING TO FEEL DEFEAT.
KLONK!
KWACK!
YIKES!
WHAT DOES GUANO MAN DO? SEND ALL OF YOU TO SIDEKICK'S PUN SCHOOL?
YOU'RE MORE IRRITATING THAN THE BOY.
WHACK!

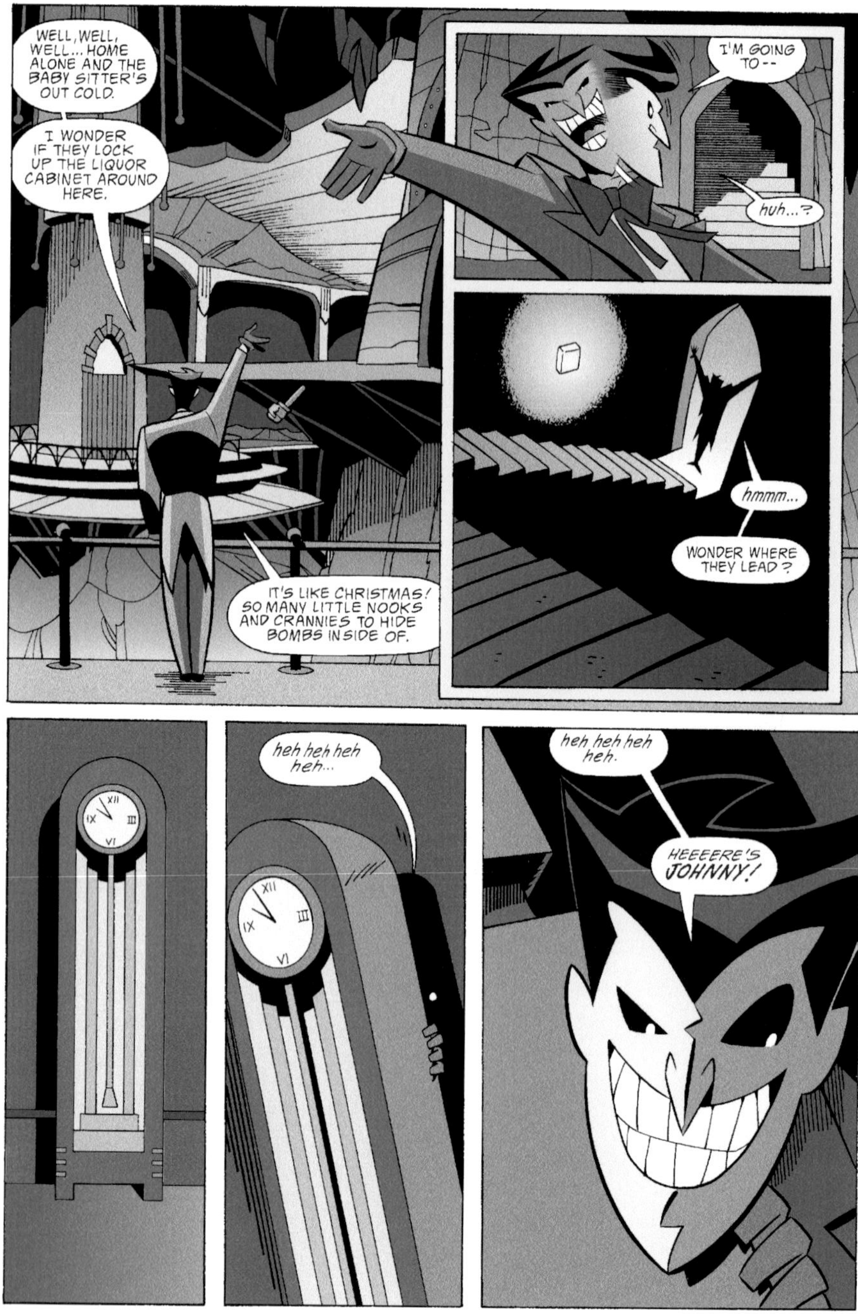

WELL, WELL, WELL... HOME ALONE AND THE BABY SITTER'S OUT COLD.
I WONDER IF THEY LOCK UP THE LIQUOR CABINET AROUND HERE.
IT'S LIKE CHRISTMAS! SO MANY LITTLE NOOKS AND CRANNIES TO HIDE BOMBS INSIDE OF.
I'M GOING TO --
huh...?
hmmm...
WONDER WHERE THEY LEAD?

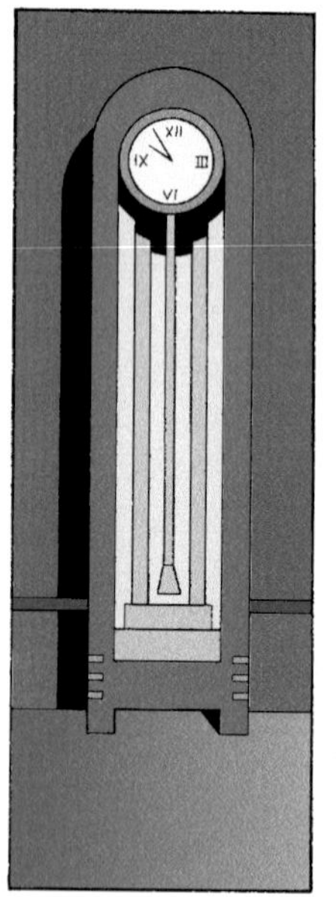

YOU'RE DOWN TO ONE LAST NUMBER, BATMAN. DON'T BE STUBBORN, IT WOULD BE A SHAME FOR OUR RELATIONSHIP TO END THIS WAY.
LAST CHANCE. WHAT DO YOU SAY?
MANEUVER 21B.
ROGER.
FWOOSH!
BETCHA YOU'RE SEEING SPOTS IN FRONT OF YOUR EYES NOW, *huh*?
LET ME HELP WITH THAT.
KLONK!

WATCH YOUR BACK, ROBIN.
POW!
KRACK
NO SWEAT. I'LL HAVE THESE GUYS WRAPPED UP IN NO TIME.
IN YOUR *FACE*, PUKE FOR BRAINS!
RIDDLER'S GONE.
VERY SHARP, CAPED CRUSADER... OBVIOUSLY I'M GOING TO HAVE TO HIRE BETTER HELP. THAT BUNCH WAS FINISHED IN TEN SECONDS FLAT.
BUT THIS IS JUST A SETBACK. I ASSURE YOU... A PAUSE IN THE MEASURE. I'M NOT DONE YET...
BATMAN, LOOK!
WHERE I'M GOING, THE ONLY WAY YOU COULD GET TO ME IS TO PRACTICE!

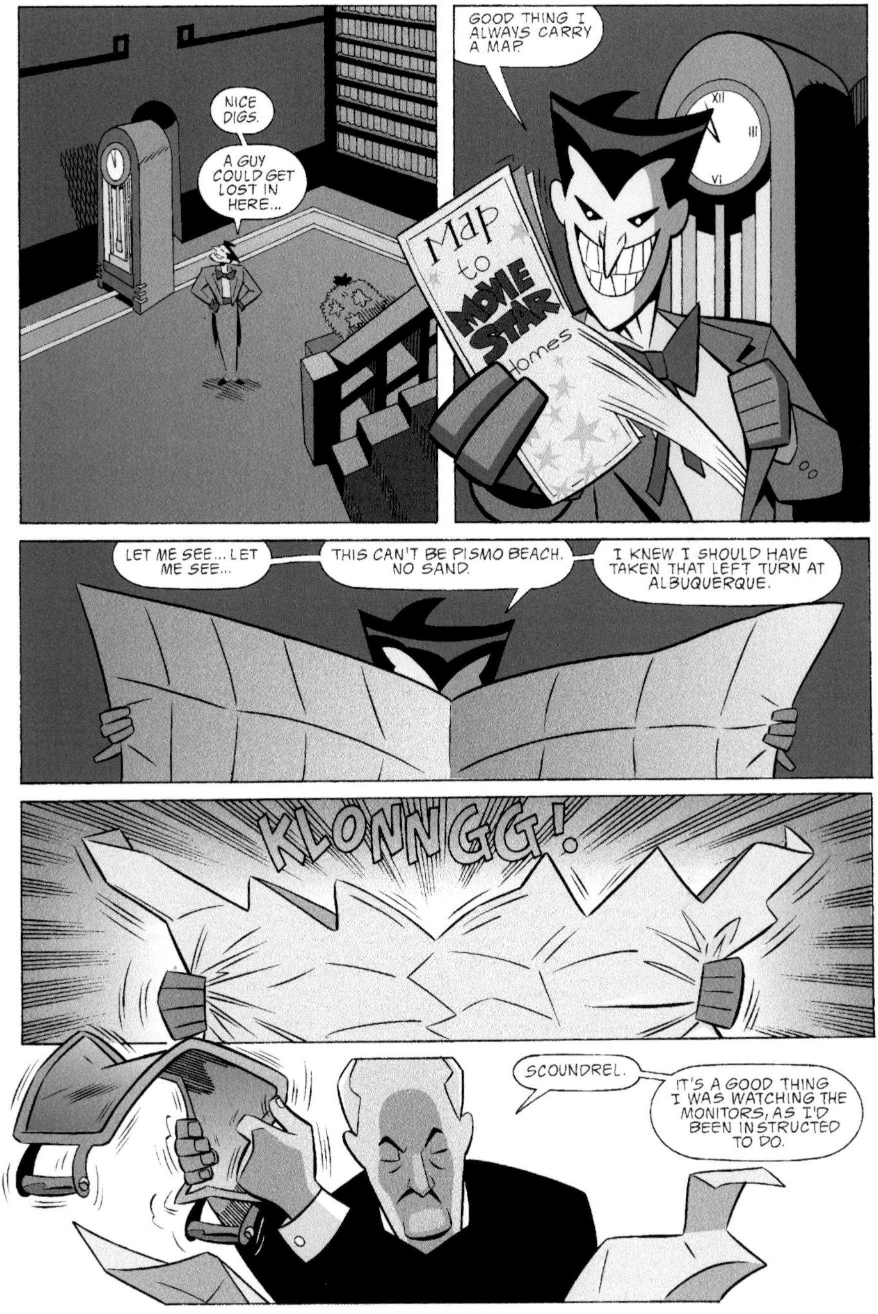

NICE DIGS.
A GUY COULD GET LOST IN HERE...
GOOD THING I ALWAYS CARRY A MAP.
Map to MOVIE STAR Homes
LET ME SEE... LET ME SEE...
THIS CAN'T BE PISMO BEACH. NO SAND.
I KNEW I SHOULD HAVE TAKEN THAT LEFT TURN AT ALBUQUERQUE.

uh...
oh MAN. BATMAN'S GOING TO HAVE MY HEAD FOR THIS ONE.
AND THE WAY IT FEELS RIGHT NOW, I'M NOT SURE I'M GOING TO WANT IT BACK.
DON'T WORRY, MISS...
I BELIEVE WE CAN KEEP THIS A PRIVATE MATTER.
THE MASTER NEED NOT KNOW.
ALFRED, YOU'RE A LIFESAVER. NOW WE HAVE TO TIE HIM BACK UP.
NOT A PROBLEM. A GENTLEMAN'S GENTLE-MAN IS ALWAYS PREPARED.
I HAVE JUST THE THING.
DUCT TAPE.

IF THE BAT IS EVER GOING TO TURN THE CLOWN IN, IT WOULD HAVE TO BE HERE...
YEAH.
REWARD
WHAT...?

STEP ASIDE, PLEASE...
SOMEBODY CAUGHT THE JOKER!
WHO'S THIS GUY?
LUCKY STIFF..

OKAY, PAL...

WE'LL TAKE IT FROM HERE.
THAT WON'T BE NECESSARY.
YOU DON'T GET IT, SHORTY...

IT WASN'T A CHOICE.
YOU KNOW, FIFTY MIL SPLITS UP BETTER IF WE SPLIT YOU UP FIRST.
SPLOOSH!
Yeesh... WHAT'S THAT?
Guhhh...
YOU RUINED MY PLANS!
ah, NO.

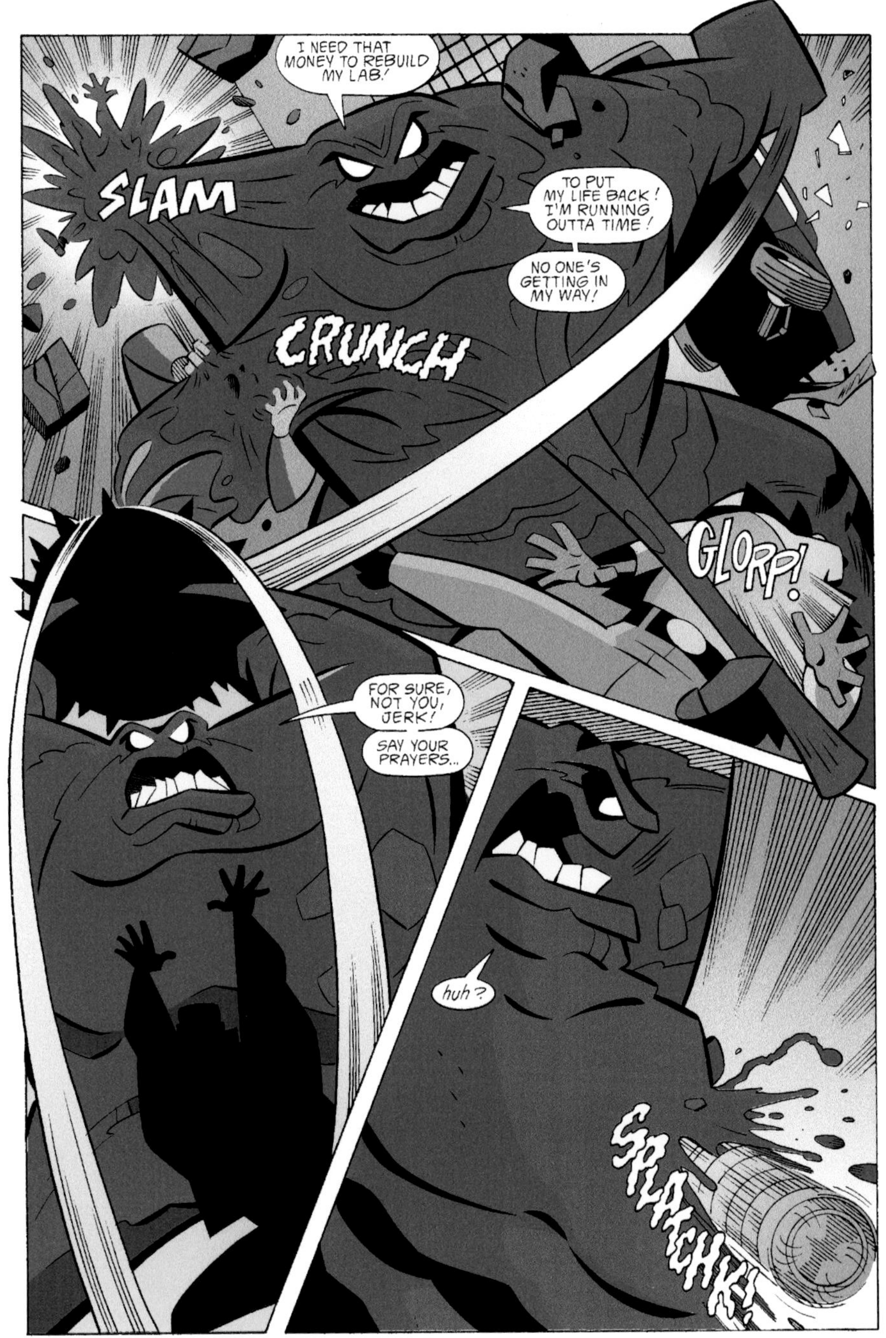
I NEED THAT MONEY TO REBUILD MY LAB!
SLAM
TO PUT MY LIFE BACK! I'M RUNNING OUTTA TIME!
NO ONE'S GETTING IN MY WAY!
CRUNCH
GLORP!
FOR SURE, NOT YOU, JERK!
SAY YOUR PRAYERS...
huh?
SPLACHK!

BELIEVE ME, CLAYFACE, I'D RATHER NOT DO THIS.
YOU'RE WAY ON THE FAR SIDE OF DISGUSTING.
BUT SOME THINGS IN LIFE, YOU JUST HAVE TO GO THROUGH.
GLITK!
HEY!
SURE HOPE THIS WORKS...

IT'S GOING TO TAKE ME A WEEK TO CLEAN OUT MY HAIR.
GET A LITTLE BIT CLOSER, SEWER LIPS...
YOU'RE GONNA PAY FOR THIS, LITTLE MAN!
PAY...?
HOW ABOUT I CHARGE IT?
KZZZZAARKT!
FRIED CLAYFACE.
blecchh...
I THINK I DISCOVERED A BRAND-NEW SMELL.

WHAT'S THAT YOU'RE TYPING...?
"THE ONLY WAY YOU COULD GET TO ME IS TO PRACTICE."
WHAT'S THAT...?
TELL ME YOU'RE NOT CROSS-REFERENCING THE WORD PRACTICE AGAINST LOCAL PLACE NAMES...
KLIK KLIK
PUHLEEEZE!
KLIK KLAK
NO TALKING.
QUIET.
ONLY YOU WOULD SOLVE A RIDDLE WITH A COMPUTER, BUTTMAN!
YOU'VE GOT THE SENSE OF HUMOR OF A ROCK.
KLIK KLAK
KLAK KLIK
LUCKY THING I'M ON THE TEAM NOW, FOR STUFF LIKE THIS.
BUT IF I HAVE TO WEAR A FLYING ANIMAL COSTUME, I WANT TO BE THE SQUIRREL.
DON'T MAKE ME GAG YOU.
IT'S ONE OF EDDIE'S LITTLE CLUES, ISN'T IT?
ooh, LET ME HELP!

YOU DO AND I'LL SUE. I HAVE THE RIGHT TO REMAIN NOISY.
I'M ALREADY PLANNING TO COME AFTER YOU FOR RESTRAINT OF TRADE.
KLIK. KLAK

IF ANYONE SHOULD BE COLLECTING ON THAT FIFTY MILLION, IT SHOULD BE ME.
YOU'D HAVE TO BE DEAD.
KLIK KLAK

DETAILS, DETAILS--I'M AN IDEA MAN.

...AND YOU'RE IGNORING ME.
KLIK KLAK KLIK

SPEAKING OF DEAD, YOU EVER WONDER WHY IT IS I'VE NEVER KILLED YOU?
NO.
I'VE BEEN DYING TO TELL YOU THIS FOR YEARS...
heeheehee hee.
KLIK KLAK
KLAK KLIK

I'VE BEEN LETTING YOU WIN.

KOOKY GAME, AIN'T IT? I CAUSE TROUBLE; YOU CATCH ME...
IF YOU WIN A ROUND, THERE'S GONNA BE A REMATCH, BUT IF I WIN ONE...
Phhtt! KAPUT!
GAME OVER.
AND WHO WANTS THAT?
SEE, BATBOOB...? I CAN TAKE YOU OUT ANY TIME YOU START TO BORE ME...
DON'T SPLASH MY WALKING SHORTS, IF YOU KNOW WHAT I MEAN...

uRK!
DESTROYING LIVES IS NOT A GAME, JOKER!
DOUGLAS REID IS A GOOD MAN!

STRUCK A NERVE, huh?
I CAN PLAY YOU LIKE A TROMBONE.

TROMBONE...?
OF COURSE.

HEY! COME BACK HERE!

"EXCUSE ME, SIR... DO YOU KNOW THE WAY TO GET TO CARNEGIE HALL?"
"PRACTICE."
"IT'S AN OLD JOKE.
CARNEGIE HAUL
MOVING AND STORAGE
FOR SALE
"CARNEGIE HAUL WAS THE TRUCKING COMPANY OWNED BY WACKO TOYS.

THEY HAD THE CONTRACT TO DISTRIBUTE RIDDLER GAMES A COUPLE OF YEARS BACK.
"RIDDLER WOULD HAVE A KEY TO THE BUILDINGS.

WHERE IS MY PHILLIPS HEAD SCREWDRIVER...?
Oh, THANK YOU.

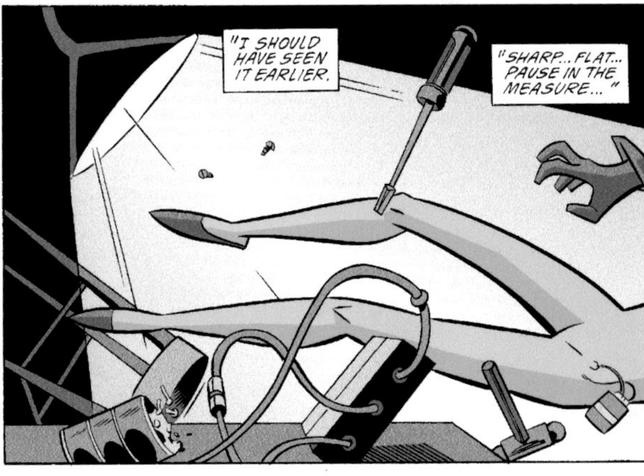
"I SHOULD HAVE SEEN IT EARLIER.
"SHARP... FLAT... PAUSE IN THE MEASURE..."

HE WAS DROPPING MUSICAL CLUES RIGHT IN FRONT OF ME ALL ALONG.
BUT I LET THE JOKER GET TO ME AND I GOT DISTRACTED.

CLAYFACE WAS MY DISTRACTION TONIGHT.
HE CAUSED A RUCKUS AT POLICE HEADQUARTERS AN HOUR AGO, LOOKING FOR THE BIG JOKER PAYOFF.
ANYONE HURT?

JUST CLAYFACE'S PRIDE.
AND A COUPLE OF PUSHY FORTUNE HUNTERS. NOTHING I COULDN'T HANDLE.

GOTHAM'S A LIT FUSE AT THE BEST OF TIMES.
THAT BOUNTY IS GOING TO MAKE IT WORSE. SOMEONE WILL GET KILLED...

UNLESS I STOP THE TROUBLE AT THE SOURCE.
STAY OUT OF THE CAVE TONIGHT, DICK.

WHO...?

WHAT THE...?
EVERY DOOR ALARM IN THE BUILDING JUST WENT OFF!
WHAT, DO WE HAVE AN ARMY BREAKING IN HERE?
BZZT
BZZT
SECURITY

MR. REID...?
oh NO...

WHERE AM I?
AT A CROSSROADS.
YOU HAVE TO CHOOSE A PATH.
heh heh.
REEDY, OLD SPROUT!
STILL UPSET WITH ME, BUDDY?
HEY, BATS, WHAT GIVES...?
YOUR BUSINESS IS MEDICINE. YOU'RE A HUMANITARIAN. YOU'VE BUILT HOSPITALS, FOOD BANKS, SHELTERS...
NO MATTER WHAT TRAGEDIES YOU'VE HAD TO SURVIVE BEFORE, YOU'VE ALWAYS CHOSEN TO DO GOOD. FOR YOURSELF AND THE PEOPLE OF THIS CITY.
IT'S TIME TO CHOOSE A PATH AGAIN, REID. DON'T LET THIS MAN DO IT FOR YOU.
I...
uh...
I WON'T ALLOW YOU TO BUY A MURDER.
IF YOU WANT THIS MAN DEAD, YOU'RE GOING TO HAVE TO CHOOSE TO KILL HIM YOURSELF.

BUT BEFORE YOU DO...
ASK YOURSELF WHAT YOU REALLY WANT...

AND IF THIS IS GOING TO DO ANY GOOD...

GET ON WITH IT!

G...G...G

NO...

NO...
I WON'T.

THE JOKER IS BACK IN CUSTODY TONIGHT AFTER G. DOUGLAS REID ANNOUNCED A RETRACTION OF THE FIFTY-MILLION-DOLLAR BOUNTY FOR THE CRIMINAL'S MURDER...
...USING THE MONEY, INSTEAD, TO CREATE THE GLENN REID FOUNDATION...
...A FUND TO BENEFIT THE VICTIMS OF VIOLENT CRIMES AND THEIR FAMILIES, HERE IN GOTHAM CITY.
HOTEL
"BE HONEST, YOU WOULD HAVE STOPPED HIM."
"I WOULDN'T HAVE HAD TO. I'VE KNOWN G. DOUGLAS REID MY WHOLE LIFE. HE WAS AN INSPIRATION TO ME GROWING UP."
HE WAS ONE OF MY FATHER'S CLOSEST FRIENDS. THERE WAS NO RISK.
YOU'RE TOO TRUSTING, BATMAN. PEOPLE ARE CAPABLE OF ANYTHING.
AT LEAST GOTHAM WILL CALM DOWN NOW.
THAT MAN DOWN THERE... RUNNING.
THINK THAT'S HIS PURSE?
DOUBTFUL.
RACE YA...
NEVER THE END

CHAPTER 1
Life in the Big Top

HALY'S CIRCUS.
OUTSIDE CHEYENNE, WYOMING.
JUNE.
Haley's
Haly's
"Ladies and gentlemen, boys and girls!
"You've traveled from across the city...
"Across the county, across the state, and beyond.
"And you've come for *one* reason..."

To be *amazed.*

From Boise to San Antonio, Missoula to Muncie, they have dazzled audiences with their breathtaking feats that defy gravity so profoundly you'll leave thinking man can *fly.*
They give something this modern world cannot— ***wonder.***
Prepare to be astonished, prepare to be thrilled as Haly's Circus proudly presents the unparalleled, the unrivaled, the one, the only...

THE FLYING GRAYSONS!

Another low turnout, Dad.
Don't worry about the crowds. Worry about the routine.
I gave up my summer for the routine. It'd be nice if people were here to see it.
Hey, at least the circus *only* travels in the summer.
Otherwise you'd be a full-time carny like your mother and father.
Right. As if that's not where my life is heading anyway.
I'm just having some fun, Dick.
Let's get this show started on one, two...

Three!

Ladies and gentlemen, there he flies!
But!

"Will...
"He...
"Make it?"

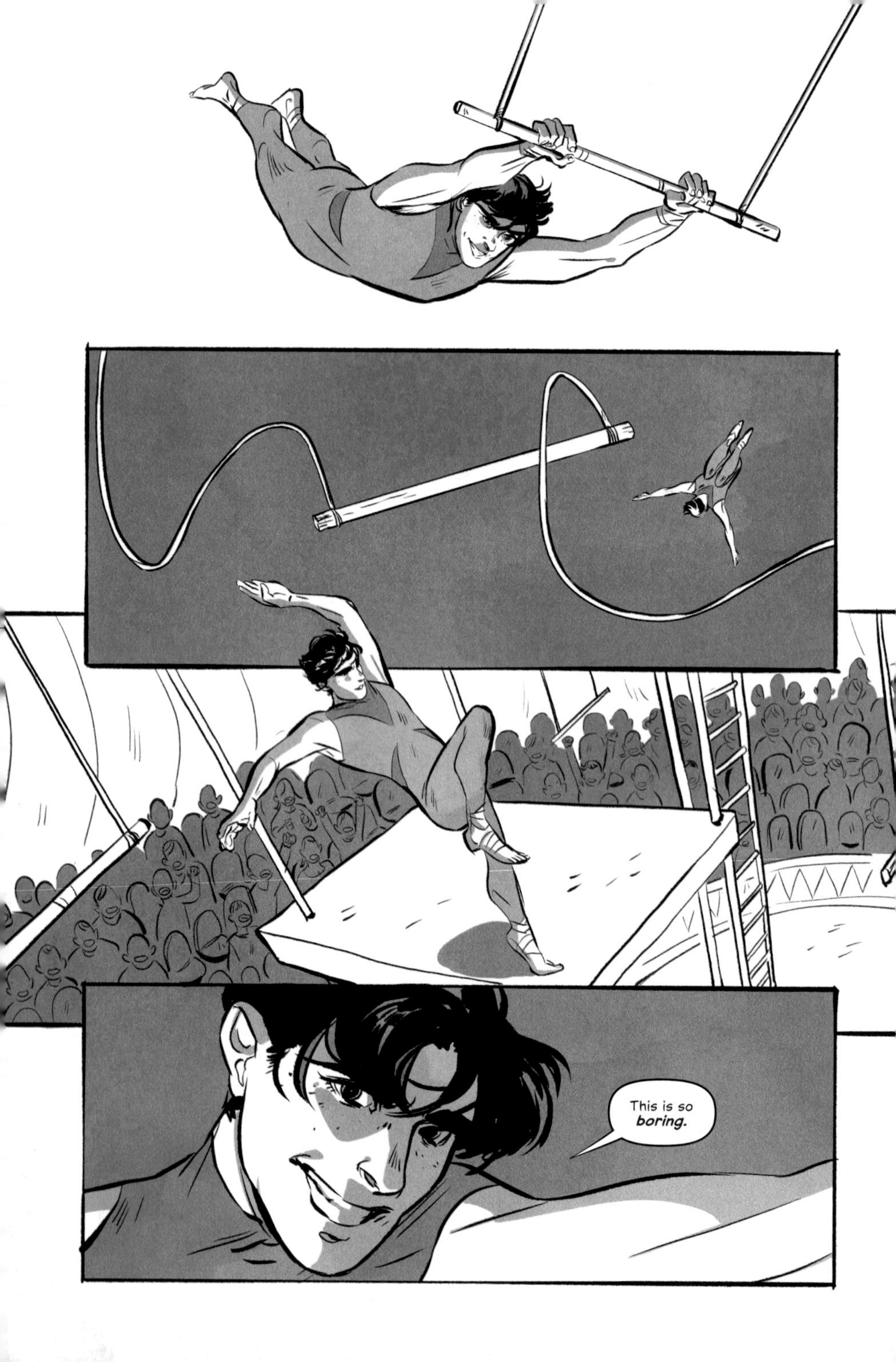
This is so *boring.*

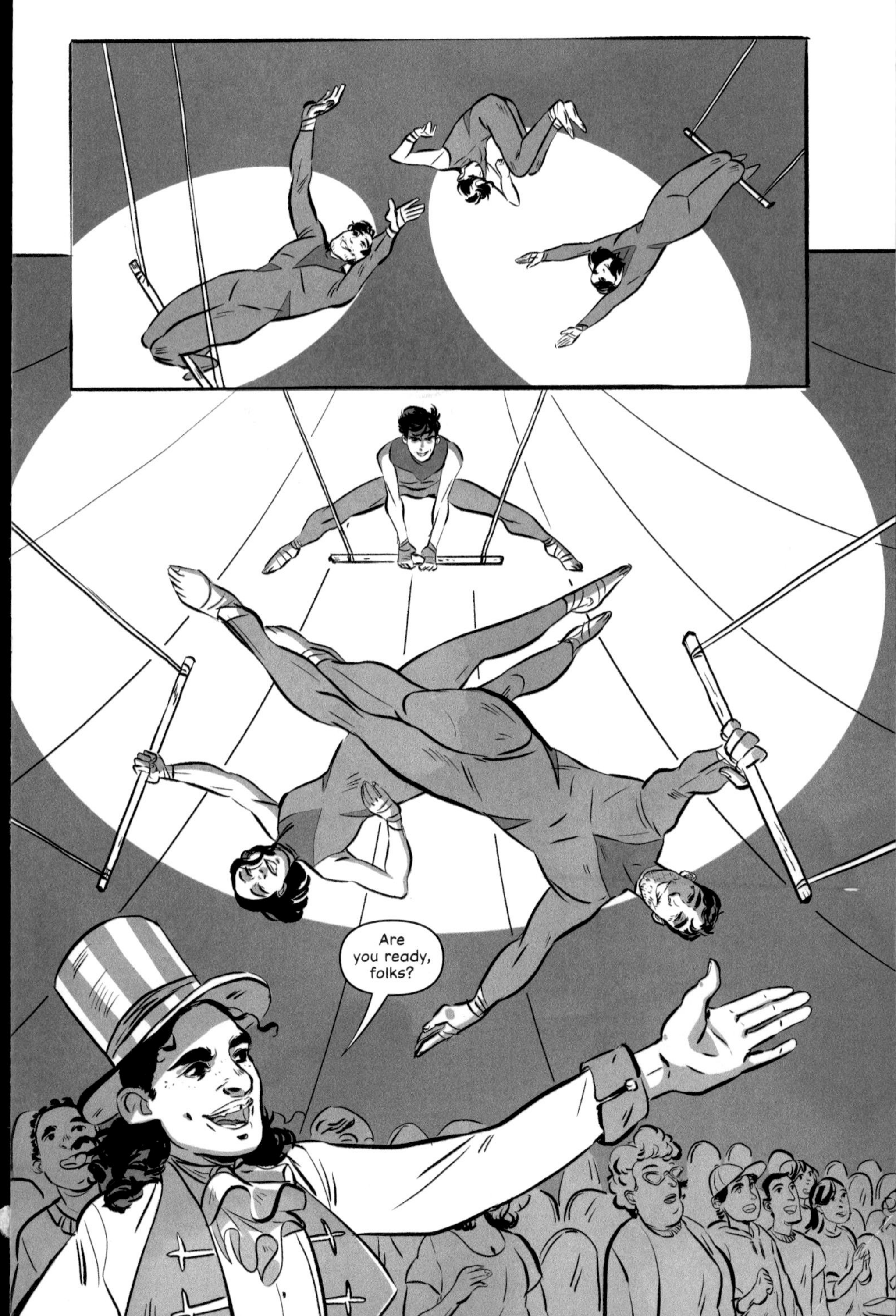
Are you ready, folks?